I0554105

Smoke Show: A Forbidden Age Gap Romance

A.D. Ryland

Published by A.D. Ryland, 2025.

SMOKE SHOW: A FORBIDDEN AGE GAP ROMANCE

First edition. August 29, 2025.

Copyright © 2025 A.D. Ryland.

ISBN: 979-8999761514

Written by A.D. Ryland.

Table of Contents

To anyone who has ever used a book to escape reality

Content Warning

One person's *yuck* is someone else's *yum*, so I decided to list all the tropes and triggers together in order to let you decide what you like, and what you don't.

Happy reading! <3

Cinnamon roll ex-con MMC

Young insecure FMC

Kidnapping

Strangers to lovers

Forbidden age gap (15 years)

Road trip

Forced proximity

One bed/One shower

Who did this to you?

Trauma bonding

Blood play/red wings

Death of family members

References to abuse including SA (Not between MCs)

References to casual drug use including OD (Not involving MCs)

Suicide/attempted suicide

Infertility due to abuse

Casual mention of incest

Light stalking

Surprise tattoos
Explicit language & graphic sexual content

Introduction

B efore you begin, I'd like to take a moment to address some of the content that lies ahead. Let me start by stating that this book was written for adults, and is a complete work of fiction– The characters, their actions, and the situations they find themselves in, are not real.

You may have noticed the word *forbidden* in reference to the age gap between my main characters. Allow me to clarify:

My FMC is just on the verge of turning eighteen. Yes, you read that correctly; she starts out at only seventeen. The legal age of consent is sixteen in Georgia, Alabama, and Mississippi (the states my MCs travel through together.)

The age discrepancy is a large plot point, so I encourage you to give it a chance, however I recognize that this is inevitably a deal-breaker for some of you.

Please know that it won't hurt my feelings if you feel the need to put this book down, and walk quickly in the opposite direction. I sincerely hope there's something else on your TBR that can scratch your itch.

However, if you dare to believe that most people are just human beings doing their best to make it in a harsh world, hoping that they're good enough to be loved, and praying that they're worthy enough to be forgiven...Then I welcome you to the Smoke Show.

Smokey

An old, rusted bell rings overhead, swinging wildly on a chain as it slams against the glass door I just pushed open into the tiny, run-down gas station. Lifting my heavy hair off the back of my neck, I feel the sweat that's already gathered between and under my breasts drip down my stomach beneath my tank top. My nipples harden under the turquoise material, and I'm grateful for the dripping and moldering air conditioner that sits lopsided in the window behind the counter, working overtime to combat the Georgia humidity in the thick of summer. The scent of old, stale grease is almost strong enough to cover that weird fart smell that clings to damp places like this.

My flip flops are loud as they take turns smacking against the dirty, yellowed floor as I walk towards the poorly stocked refrigerated section. Each time I lift a foot to take a step, I can feel the bottoms of my flimsy, pink sandals peeling off of the permanently sticky linoleum. Trusty Rusty'z has been like this for as long as I can remember which, admittedly, isn't very long.

Continuing past the meager selection of Red Bull, Coke, Dr. Pepper, sweet tea, and water, I stop in front of the fully stocked shelves of beer. This place is always dependable for

1

something at least. That's why Uncle Mike lets me come here. They always have what he needs.

"*And so do you, Sugar.*"

Squeezing my eyes shut, I shake my head back and forth as if I can dislodge his ugly voice with the action.

If only.

With a resigned sigh, I open the cold glass door to grab a six pack, wishing I could climb inside the cool interior, rather than return to the sweltering summer heat for the trek back home.

Home. Now there's a concept.

I snort quietly, holding a mental conversation with myself as I make my way to the counter, so I don't pay any attention to the man who enters when the little bell goes wild above the door again. I don't want to see the way his eyes crawl over me in the few seconds it takes us to pass each other.

I'm no stranger to the way men notice my curves. And my bruises. I'd cover up more to hide them, but then I'd die of heat stroke or something, and also, fuck that! Enough has already been taken from me without adding the comfort of breezy clothing to that list. At least no one can see the scars. People would never stop gawking at me then.

"Hey, Lenny," I say mildly, placing the cardboard carrier of Busch on the counter. "Just here for the usual."

"O-kay do-kay, Mizz Smokey," he says, tossing a package of Marlboro Reds next to the beer, before flashing me his gap-toothed grin. He says the same thing every time, his accent causing him to pronounce my name like *Smoke-AY,* instead of *Smoke-EY.*

God, this place is predictable. But I smile back, because at least Lenny has always been kind to me. He even sells me "the usual" beer and cigarettes even though he knows I'm underage. But he also knows that he's saving me some more of these bruises. Besides, it's not like Trusty Rusty'z is at the top of anyone's inspection list. Sometimes he even gives me a free bottle of water when the heat index is so high, his little window unit can't keep up with cooling this little, rinky-dink place down.

I hand him a wad of exact change after I peel it from the sweaty pocket of my black jean shorts.

"Until next time," I turn to leave, giving Lenny a little wave without looking back.

The bell dances manically against the glass door as it swings shut behind me.

The hot Georgia sun beats down on my head when I stop on the crumbling sidewalk outside the door. Cicadas scream from the trees across the highway while the air above the asphalt bounces up and down in blurry little waves from the intense heat. I try taking a deep breath, but the air is so hot and thick, there's little relief from the action. My gaze drops to the frosty six-pack in my left hand, already dripping with condensation.

For a moment it appears to grow larger, like an anchor weighing me down to this sad and empty life. What's stopping me from running? My incompetent step-mother and her deadbeat brother tell me I should be grateful that they allow me to walk alone from our shitty little trailer park to the middle-of-nowhere gas station. The sad thing is, I am.

The Peach Pit is situated just a few miles down the dirt road out behind Trusty Rusty'z, and I've always cherished the solitude of the long walk despite the boiling atmosphere. Relished the moments without stale beer and cigarette smoke clogging up my lungs, and hateful vitriol being spewed at me while I'm treated like an ashtray. But most of all, I rejoice in the absence of my twisted uncle's heavy hands roaming my body.

So why do I always go back?

Where else would you go?

His sick voice counters in my mind. I'm not yet eighteen, though that problem will solve itself in just a few more months. For what has to be more than the millionth time, I curse my mother for being able to escape this life, and my dad for dying and leaving me with these monsters.

I pull my gaze up from the brown glass bottles to the barren horizon, feeling overwhelmed with hopelessness. Because the truth is there isn't anywhere else for me to go.

The rhythmic clank of the rusty, metal bell dangling from the door behind me pulls me from my desolate thoughts, as well as announces the presence of the man who stops beside me. His shadow dwarfs mine on the cracked sidewalk. Out of the corner of my eye, I watch his thick, tattooed arms as he taps a pack of Newports against his palm before cracking the top open, and placing one of the thin white cylinders between his lips. Flipping the little rectangle closed, he deposits it in a back pocket, and when his hand reappears, there's a smaller box rattling in his palm.

His eyes flick to me suddenly, catching me watching him as he slides the insert out of its sleeve like a little drawer, and selects a match. Without breaking eye contact, he strikes the little red tip against the side of the box, sparking the flame to life. And just like a fire needs oxygen, I remind myself to take a breath as he cups his big hand around the little orange flame and carefully marries it to the end of his cigarette. The cherry glows bright as he inhales.

"Problem?" A cloud of smoke escorts the deep, raspy word out of his throat.

His voice has a smooth, southern cadence, but I can tell he's not from around here. It causes my brain to short circuit for a moment before I notice that my lip is curled in disgust at the gray stream of pollution trailing from the end of the slender white stick. Clearing my throat before looking at him, I try to smooth out my expression.

"I-I just don't like cigarettes," I say, shaking my hair back, trying not to think about all the reasons why. His gaze drops to look pointedly at the pack of Marlboro Reds I'm still clutching in my other hand. My eyes follow his, and I clear my throat nervously, again.

"These aren't for me," I explain quickly, for no reason. I don't owe this guy anything. This absurdly large, beautiful man.

He's so tall I have to tilt my head back to get a look at his face, or else I'd just be staring at the wall of his chest. His broad, expansive chest that grows larger each time he inhales, taking a drag of his cigarette. Honestly, I should feel intimidated by him, but for some reason I don't.

He wears a dingy, white backwards ball-cap that keeps his sun-streaked hair out of his face, while his eyes are a complimentary deep, warm brown. They may be the most comforting eyes I've ever had the pleasure of gazing into. Like rich mugs of hot chocolate on a cold winter day. Not that I have much experience with those. Mugs of hot chocolate, or cold winters.

As I continue to drink him in, I study his mustache and short beard, noticing they both contain subtle hints of silver streaked throughout. I wonder briefly what the shiny, red-tinted strands would feel like between my fingertips. Would they be thick and coarse, as they appear? Or maybe they're deceptively silky and soft.

"Are you waiting for someone?"

The question rolls over me in a cloud of smoke, pulling me from the inappropriate and alarming direction of my thoughts. The facial hair does an exceptional job at disguising his age. He could be twenty-five or forty for all I know.

He's looking at me expectantly as he draws on his cigarette. Is it smart to be honest here and say no? Should I answer yes instead?

"I don't live far." I settle for a vague truth.

At my response, he looks around at the deserted landscape. There's nothing to see but the forgotten two-lane highway, the trees filled with trilling insect life, two sad, little gas pumps off to the right, and a big, black semi truck hauling an empty trailer parked beside them. When his eyes meet mine again, I can tell he doesn't believe me.

"Everything is far from here, Liv." The right corner of his mouth curls into a crooked half smile that reveals what could be a dimple winking in his left cheek, though it's a little hard to tell through his facial hair. I'm so lost in looking at him, I barely even notice the lazy way he calls me someone else's name.

"Can I give you a ride?"

The inquiry, not said unkindly or in a threatening way, still hits me like a bucket of ice water. Only metaphorically, of course, since I can still unfortunately feel sweat trickling across my scalp.

My eyes snap back over to the black semi that has to be his, since nobody else is here with us. Besides Lenny, of course, but I already know what his old, beat to hell pick-up looks like. I pass it on my way here every time I come, parked out around back.

I allow myself a moment to fantasize about accepting his offer. I could ditch this albatross of brown bottles dangling from my hand and hop up into his truck, allowing him to take me away from my own personal Hell. I could escape. I could be free. I could leave all this misery behind.

But on the heels of that fantasy, I picture a life worse than the one I already have. This man is a complete and total stranger to me. His size alone should be frightening. Just because he feels inexplicably safe, and appears to have kind eyes that can see to the very brokenness inside my soul doesn't mean it's smart to trade the Devil I know for one that I don't. So to speak.

"No, thanks!" I finally force out, too quick and too bright, before stepping off the curb and walking away, trying not to think about what could happen if he decides to follow me.

Jackson

I watch her expressions carefully, noting the uncertainty in her pretty, blue eyes when I ask if she's waiting for someone. It's a struggle not to smile when I see the full blown panic cross her face after I offer to give her a ride.

I can tell she's young, though her actual age is hard to discern. She's got a carrier of beer in one hand, and a pack of cigarettes in the other, so I at least know she's legal. Her looks remind me of my first crush, Liv Tyler, in that old movie about saving the world from an asteroid apocalypse or something. What was the name of it again? Oh yeah. *Armageddon.*

Only this girl's eyes are brighter, appearing more turquoise than blue, though they could just look that way because of the color of her top, and the shadow of the fading bruise I can spy around her left eye-socket. Alarm bells start going off in my mind as that realization sinks in, a sure sign that I'm probably about to do something stupid. In a bid to keep myself relaxed and under control, I lift my hand to take another puff off my cigarette as I casually observe the rest of her features.

Her mouth is wide and plump, like it was made for sucking cock. The split in her bottom lip only enhances the image in my mind, though I'm not exactly proud of it.

Sizing her up, I think she actually has a little more to offer a man than Liv Tyler ever did. I'm trying my hardest not to stare too much at her chest, but the way her sweat glistens in the sunlight highlights her considerable cleavage.

Get a fucking grip, Jackson.

I mentally scold myself to focus. I've been out of prison long enough to have more goddamn self-control than this. Surely I can keep it together and not lose my head over a pretty mouth and a great rack. Especially when they come attached to a girl that, legal or not, is obviously way too young for me. I have made it my personal mission in life to be nothing like my father was, and drooling over jail bait hits too close to home.

Belated shame and disgust wash over me, combatting my lustful thoughts as I continue to stare at her. The assorted bruises, and cigarette burns that I can see decorating her otherwise creamy flesh fuel a hatred inside of me I've been trying to bury for too long. Recognizing this, I'm unsure if I'll be able to leave her alone the way I know I should.

She gazes at my truck with a longing I shouldn't understand, but I do. She's looking at it like it could be the solution to all her problems in this world. Like she might just take me up on my offer, but instead of taking her home, she'll beg me to save her from it.

My jaw flexes as I grit my teeth when I consider the lost look on her face, her many visible injuries, and the reasons why she would have them. Taking the time to do a slow count to five in my head, I work on forcing myself to calm down. When she does finally answer me, she quickly rejects my offer before turning and walking the other way. Despite myself, my mouth twitches with a hint of appreciation. *Smart girl.*

She puts distance between us, one flimsy, pink sandaled foot at a time, and I stay rooted to the spot, hating myself as I admire her shapely figure and finish smoking my cigarette. Watching her form shrink, I can't help but speculate over her bruised face and busted lip, recalling the desperate way she stared at my truck. It was as if she were envisioning another life, one far away from here, and I allow myself to remember what I did the last time a pair of sad, blue eyes begged me for my help. Or rather what I didn't do.

The guilt still eats at me after all these years, and it's hard not to see this broken, abused girl as a golden opportunity to make up for my past mistakes. It would be a risky decision, I know, but the ghosts haunting me seem pleased by the thought.

With my mind made up, I drop what's left of my cigarette and snuff it out with the tip of my steel-toed boot before strolling over to my truck. Other than the USDOT number on the side of my door, there are no defining marks, brands, or logos to set Black Betty apart from any other black semi trucks out there on the road. And that's exactly how I like it.

Climbing up into the driver seat, I switch my ball cap around and pull it down low to hide my face. There's no one around to witness what I'm about to do except for the cashier inside, and he seems a few beers short of a six-pack, if you know what I mean. Even still, it's better to be safe than sorry.

As I put the truck into drive, I pause for a moment, before letting off the brake.

Are you really going to do this? I hesitate, doubting myself.

"*Is there any other way?*" Amy's voice counters from the darkness in my mind, mocking me. Closing my eyes, I do a slow countdown from five in my head, working to remain in control of my emotions.

This isn't right. What if I'm wrong about her? I try one last time to appeal to the logical, sane part of my brain.

"What if you're not?"

I don't have a response to offer myself because I know from experience that those bruises don't lie.

"Do for her what you should have done for me."

Amy's voice echoes again, inflaming my sense of guilt, but giving me the permission I need to trust my gut and follow my instincts, however misguided they may seem.

With my conscience temporarily nullified, I finally ease off the brake, heading down the little back road behind the curvy Liv Tyler look-alike.

Smokey

For a while, I'm comforted by the lack of footsteps behind me until I hear the rumble of an engine start up and slowly grow louder as if growing closer. Peering over my shoulder, I confirm that the black truck is indeed lumbering toward me, causing my heartbeat to kick up into double time. The guy from Rustyz is actually following me!

I do the only thing I can think of to do, which is to drop the beer and pick up my pace. Brown glass shatters, spilling cool liquid, turning dirt to mud under my poorly clad feet as I begin moving from left to right in a frenzied zig zag pattern. It doesn't matter that it doesn't make any logical sense to try and outrun a vehicle that's capable of speeding up and, not only catching me, but running me over. What else am I supposed to do, though? Just let some stranger take me? My life may be shit, but it's still the only one I've ever known.

When I hear the truck stop behind me, a gasp of relief bursts from my lungs just before a hard body tackles me to the ground, knocking the air and premature triumph out of me. Fuck, he moves insanely fast for a giant. He probably still would've caught me even without the truck.

No! I shove the hopeless thought away the same way I attempt to shove him, but the precious seconds I lost stunned by his impact have cost me too much. He's already clamped a firm hand over my mouth and begun dragging me like a rag doll towards the open door of the waiting vehicle, my additional weight not appearing to hinder his speed and agility in the slightest.

"HELP!" I throw myself across the cab of the truck to the passenger side, immediately fumbling with the handle as I scream for someone, anyone to save me. Of course the door is already locked with no visible way for me to unlock it by hand.

Trembling, I try to fight back the panic and not let the fear overwhelm me, but I can't help it. It's actually happening. I'm actually being kidnapped!

I ignore the small flower of relief that blooms somewhere deep inside me, and try to focus on the very real danger I'm in. This isn't a fantasy or a daydream anymore. This is my real life. Whatever is left of it, anyway.

Unwanted tears stream down my cheeks as I pound my fists against the window, as if I have the strength to break the glass with my bare hands.

"Please let me out, let me go!" I beg over and over, my voice growing hoarse and weakening along with my physical efforts as helplessness begins to consume me.

"Are you done yet?" The voice that was sending pleasurable tingles down my spine just a few short minutes ago, now sends ripples of trepidation through me.

"Am I *done*?" I cut back in sheer, unadulterated exasperation. It must be adrenaline making me so brave. "I've been waiting my whole damn life to be done! *Done* with hateful women who leave me behind, or treat me like gum that they can't wait to scrape off the bottom of their shoe. *Done* with the shitty entitlement of men; no not men, *boys,* who think no means yes, and that force is a form of foreplay," I pin him with a look of sheer disgust before continuing my spiral. "*Done* with the never ending pain and disappointment of being a living waste of space that nobody seems to care about, so YES, I'M FUCKING *DONE*!!!" I scream like a full blown lunatic, tearing at my hair while tears and snot mingle in a stream down my face.

Nothing but silence and the sound of my labored breathing fill the cab after my outburst.

"Please," I finally croak, stopping to swallow around the massive knot that has formed in my throat. "There's nothing you can do to me that I haven't already experienced." I hate the way my voice begins to shake, but I press on anyway. "I-If you're going to kill me...Please, just get it over with." I look over at him solemnly. "I've suffered enough. You'd honestly be doing me a favor."

I notice the way his grip tightens on the steering wheel, but he doesn't meet my gaze.

"I'm so tired," I finish in a broken whisper, turning away to stare hopelessly out the window.

Jackson

She cries in my passenger seat, cutting me open with all the skill and precision of a surgeon. Gutting me with every word. I knew I wasn't wrong about the abuse she was enduring, but it's disconcerting to have her confirm it by asking so casually for her death. She's even more broken than I thought, vindicating my impulsive decision to take her— save her. My only regret is the way she fears me. I never meant to frighten her, though in hindsight, I guess I don't really know what else I expected.

"I have no interest in killing you, Liv," I tell her as I carefully reverse back out onto the vacant highway. She snorts in disbelief as she wipes her nose on the inside of her arm. "I mean it." I try to sound reassuring. "I only want to help you."

"By abducting me?" Her tone is incredulous. "Yeah, okay. That definitely sends a '*helpful*' message."

She makes air quotes with her fingers when she says the word helpful, and I can't stop the little chuckle that slips past my lips as I watch her eyes sparkle with defiance. She may think she's ready to die, but the way she spits venom at me would suggest otherwise.

"You think this is *funny*?" She asks, still beyond upset.

"Not at all," I answer with a smile as I put the truck into drive and begin putting as much distance between her and this God-forsaken place as possible.

Casting my eyes her way, I try not to be obvious in my scrutiny of her. She has her knees drawn up to her chest with her arms wrapped around them in a defensive position. Splatters of mud dot her calves from when she dropped the beer, and I spot a thin trickle of red along the outside of her left ankle where the glass must have nicked her. The sight of her blood has my groin tightening and I tell myself that I'll need to stop and get the first aid kit out soon. She's also going to need new shoes, since the useless pieces of pink plastic she had on her feet are back in the dust. Along with all the broken glass.

Leaving evidence like that wasn't smart. I was so focused on grabbing her and getting away that I didn't think about anything else. I'll have to be on alert and extra careful for a little while, but since I don't intend to keep her, what we left behind is the least of my worries. Right now, I need to concentrate on making sure the unintended cargo I just stole knows that she's safe with me.

She sits facing away from me, staring out the passenger-side window while her curtain of dark hair hides most of her body from me. She looks so damn much like Amy, my chest aches, and thanks to the painful lessons my old man taught me, I can read her like a book. She acts like she's trying to draw inside of herself and make herself smaller. Like she's afraid to take up space. Afraid to exist and have needs, because she's only ever been an object to use to satisfy someone else's. Unable to stomach the thought of her being afraid of *me*, I try to diffuse the tension growing between us.

"You don't have to believe me," I tell her, "I know you don't know me from Adam, but I don't want to hurt you. At all." I glance in her direction again, but besides the occasional sniffle, she doesn't move. Determined to put her at ease, I go on. "I just want..." I pause for a moment because I have no right to want anything when it comes to her. We're strangers to each other. But I know what abuse looks like. When you've survived it, you can recognize it in someone else. And I can't ignore those signs, again. I can't stand by and do nothing. Especially not when it seems like I'm getting a second chance to save my dear, sweet Amy.

"I just want you to be safe." I finally finish my statement from earlier. "And I kinda got the feeling back there that maybe..." I pause again and look to her for any type of encouragement, but her body language still offers me nothing. At least she's not kicking and screaming and begging to get away anymore. I'll consider that a point in my favor at least.

"I just got the feeling that you were looking for a way out and, well... I acted on it." I return my eyes to the road when she still doesn't move or say anything. "I admit, it's probably not my most thought out plan, but—" She snorts sarcastically and I have to fight another smile, relieved that she's listening to me at all. "But there it is." I finish, and the statement hangs in the air between us. The muted sound of the road is all that rewards my explanation.

With a heavy sigh I reach forward to flip the radio on, dispelling the heavy silence, and she flinches as I execute the motion like she expected me to hit her. An old country song about love and loss fills the cab while I grip the steering wheel so tight it creaks under my hands, reminding me to go through another slow five count in my head.

I've never hit a woman before. Not one who didn't want me to, at least. But it's not like *she* knows that. Even though I just proclaimed my noble intent for taking her, I wouldn't trust me either based on whatever horrors she's already seen and experienced.

Not anymore though, I think valiantly to myself, strengthening my resolve as my hands flex and relax on the wheel.

Never again.

I'll get her somewhere safe, where she can start her life over, and then maybe I'll finally be able to sleep at night.

Smokey

We've been driving for a while now, and he hasn't tried to do anything to me since he tackled me and forced me up into his truck. My eyelids are starting to feel heavy in the absence of the adrenaline rush from earlier, but I have to stay alert. Even though he claims to be some sort of savior, he could just be waiting for the right moment to pounce again, and I'll be damned if I'm going to give him one. I won't let him catch me off guard again.

I've been thinking of ways to escape, even considering causing him to swerve and crash into the trees that line either side of the road, but that seems too risky. I could get hurt or killed in the process as well, and I'm not sure that's the smartest plan. He's got to stop eventually though, right? For gas, or food, or to use the bathroom? Maybe I can try to get away then.

As if God Himself heard my thoughts, I feel the truck slowing down as he pumps the brakes and pulls off the road into a gravel parking lot outside of a rustic little diner located in the middle of nowhere. The type of place where the food is probably delicious as long as you don't ask any questions and no one tells you what you're actually eating. My stomach growls just thinking about it, and now that we've stopped, I allow myself to acknowledge the growing discomfort in my bladder.

He puts the large vehicle into park, then drops his hands into my lap without turning it off or making a move to get out. He sits, staring out the windshield, and I try my best to sit quietly and be patient. But if we sit here any longer, I'm going to pee all over myself and stain his seat.

"Uhmm..." I start with uncertainty, and it's like the sound of my voice pulls some kind of trigger because suddenly he's moving, turning the keys and getting out of the truck. Dumbfounded, I sit and watch him round the front, before he yanks the passenger side door open. With him standing outside on the ground, and me still sitting up in the truck, his face is perfectly level with my thighs.

Our gazes collide for just a second as he reaches underneath my seat and pulls out a white, plastic square box with a faded red cross on the front. It's obviously a first aid kit. I don't know what's happening or what I should do, so I just continue to sit frozen like fucking Bambi in a set of headlights. Setting the box on the floorboard by my feet, he uses both his thumbs to pop the lid off, so he can paw through the contents within.

The next thing I know, warm, strong fingers wrap around my left ankle, and an embarrassing squeak squeezes its way out of my throat at the unexpected contact. Suppressing another one of those annoyingly endearing cocky smiles, he pulls my foot toward him a little, and only then do I notice the small, stinging wound on the outside of my leg.

Flustered, I watch him lift a packaged antiseptic wipe up to his mouth, and his velvety brown eyes find mine again just as he rips the paper with his teeth. For a moment, it looks like he could be ripping open a condom, in a hurry to get it on with his eager lover, and my breath catches in my throat before I get a hold of myself.

His eager lover? Are you serious right now, Smokey?

I try to swallow as I mentally scold myself, but my mouth has suddenly gone dry.

Seemingly unaware of the havoc he's wreaking on my nervous system, he removes the little wet wipe from its wrapper, and I watch enthralled as he not only gently cleans the cut, but blows on it tenderly to ease the burn when I let out a hiss in discomfort.

I am completely baffled by this man right now. Sure, he took me. Ran me down with his big, black truck before he tackled me and forced me up into the vehicle. And that was scary as all Hell, I won't lie. I thought I was finally looking down the cold, hard barrel of the end. But he hasn't made a single move since then to hurt me, or even *touch* me until now, and he's...trying to heal me.

He finishes up by rubbing some type of ointment over the laceration, and then smoothing a bandaid over it. Dropping the ointment back into the box, he presses the lid down onto it, then tucks it back out of sight.

"Listen, Liv" he starts, readjusting his dingy hat, and I wonder briefly why he keeps calling me that. "I know that your instincts are probably screaming at you to run. To get the hell away from me as fast as you possibly can." He looks at me steadily as if gauging my reaction. I do my best to keep my expression neutral, giving nothing away because *of fucking course* I want to run.

Don't I?

I ignore that thought, and try to listen over my pounding heartbeat.

"In order to deter that," he goes on, "I'm going to hold your hand as we walk together inside, and we're going to act like any other couple just passing through for a bite to eat." I feel my cheeks heat at the implication of us being together like that, and look away from him as he continues.

"We're going to walk in there..." as he talks, he pulls out an absurdly large pair of black and white slides, placing them on the floor board in front of me. Only then do I realize that my flip-flops are missing. "...and because I'm a gentleman, I'll even walk you to the restroom." I would laugh at his high opinion of himself if my need for the bathroom wasn't so pressing. Before I can slide my feet into his oversized sandals, he adds, "And I really hope you won't try to get away, Liv." He catches my gaze. "You already know that I'm faster than you."

"Maybe hiding behind an engine," I spit back before I can stop myself. Like a reflex, past experience and self preservation have me quickly pressing a hand to my lips to keep any further outbursts from spilling out. I hate the way his eyes sparkle as his stupid mouth quirks into that crooked little grin, so I narrow my eyes at him to silently communicate my displeasure. I meant what I said even if I didn't mean to say it.

"I'd be happy to provide another demonstration of how good I am at catching and subduing you, little girl. Maybe I'll even let you take the fall this time." His eyes heat as they rake over my body, and I can feel their warmth raising goosebumps across my flesh as he adds, "I'd love the chance to get you under me again."

My only response is an audible swallow to punctuate the avid burning in my cheeks. I should feel afraid. Repulsed, even. Instead, a thread of excitement runs through me at his words. *He wants me.* Maybe I can use that to my advantage. If he wants me, then he won't hurt me. Not in any ways that are new to me at least.

He grasps my hand to help me down from the truck, his grip firm enough to make the bones in my hand ache as they grind uncomfortably against one another. Walking in his giant shoes proves to be more of an obstacle than either of us bargained for, but true to his word, he doesn't let go or ease up on the pressure one bit as we approach the front doors. He doesn't even let go once we're inside. As soon as he locates the bathrooms, he's hauling me in that direction, pushing into the ladies room before me.

"What are you doing?" I blurt out. "You can't be in here!" I try to yank my hand from his, but it only increases the pressure from uncomfortable to painful before he lets me go a moment later.

"You want to share a stall, too?" I bite at him, forgetting all my self-preservation skills while I shake my hand out, flexing my fingers.

"I was just making sure you won't be able to climb out a window or something," he supplies. "But don't tempt me, Liv." He winks at me on his way out, and again, I feel that inexplicable thread tugging at my core.

Grateful for his absence, I relieve myself in peace. After washing my hands, I rest them on either side of the sink and stare at my reflection. My cheeks are flushed and my hair looks like a rat's nest. I tongue the split in my lip, wincing a little at the slight sting, which draws my attention to the healing bruise around my left eye. Did I kid myself into thinking he wants me? I snort as I turn away from the mirror, sick of looking at the pale, disheveled girl with too many bruises. *Some temptress I am.* How else can I get out of this, though?

I could go out there and make a scene; let everyone know that I am not willingly with whoever that man is out there. Lord knows my appearance would help sell the performance. Someone might even call the cops, and this whole nightmare would be over.

My stomach flips with uncertainty. *This* nightmare would end, but then I'd just get sent right back to the old one.

Is that really what you want?

With a sigh, I pump the well-worn lever of the paper towel dispenser until there's a thin curtain of brown paper hanging just above the floor. Wadding it all up, I wet it down so I can wipe myself off from the involuntary roll in the dirt I took earlier. Sadly, there's nothing I can do to save my ruined shirt.

Exiting the bathroom, I walk straight into a warm, solid wall of tattooed muscle wearing a dirty t-shirt. There's a small amount of pleasure in acknowledging his clothes are ruined too.

Without a word, he takes my hand again, escorting me across the sparsely occupied restaurant over to a booth situated in a corner beneath the front windows, giving us a perfect view of my new prison in the parking lot. He slides onto the wooden bench seat beside me, caging me in instead of claiming the one across from me as I had hoped and expected.

An impatient waitress in a grease stained apron shuffles over immediately to take our drink order: Dr. Pepper for him, and iced tea for me. This is the South, so I don't have to ask for it to be sweet. It would be un-American to drink it any other way.

"Why do you call me Liv?" I ask to dispel the heavy silence we seem to be stuck in after the waitress has waddled away.

He smiles before he responds with his own question. "Have you ever seen the movie *Armageddon* with Ben Affleck and Bruce Willis?"

"No?" I answer as if it should be obvious.

Shaking his head, he continues to grin.

"Then you wouldn't understand."

"Whatever." I cross my arms and roll my eyes, annoyed with his non-answer, and the way he keeps smiling. *At least one of us is having a good time,* I think sourly to myself.

The waitress returns with our beverages and places them on the table in front of us.

"Ya'll ready tuh orda?" she asks irritably, pulling a notepad out of the pocket of her soiled apron.

"We actually haven't even looked at the menu yet, ma'am, I'm sorry." He offers her his patented, dimple-popping smile, and I watch the older woman's cranky attitude dissolve faster than a drop of water on the hot, Georgia sidewalk.

"No problem, honey, take all the time ya need." She bats her eyelashes at him before ambling away again.

"I could call you something else if I knew your name." He says pointedly in her absence, but when I hesitate, he sighs. "You can call me Jackson."

Jackson

"Smokey," she supplies quietly before taking a sip of her sweet tea.

"It's a pleasure to meet you, Smokey." I look her in the eye as I taste her name for the first time. I want her to know that I mean it. "I apologize if my actions up to this point have been... frightening." She snorts into her drink at this, but I continue anyway. "I hope that you learn to trust me before this is all over."

She watches me intently for a moment, spinning the red, plastic cup between her fingers in what appears to be a nervous gesture as her impossibly blue eyes move back and forth between mine. Suddenly her expression shifts, and she looks almost playful when she fires back, "Don't hold your breath. Also," she continues, lifting a hand to motion between the two of us. "What is... *this,* exactly? Why did you..." She drops her gaze to the table top, hesitating. "Why did you take me?"

Amy's face swims to the surface of my mind, but I push it away, my leg bouncing in agitation.

"I could just tell you needed help. That you wanted to run away from something." I shrug my shoulders noncommittally. "I've been there before."

Desperate to change the subject and to learn more about her I ask, "How old are you?" The question seems to catch her off guard, causing her eyebrows to pinch together for a moment like she has to think about the answer.

"Twenty," she replies, before turning away to grab the sticky menus that rest between the window and the napkin dispenser.

I'm relieved by her answer. She's still too young for me, but a line of tension eases between my shoulder blades nonetheless. It's comforting to have confirmation that she's not a minor. I'm not like my old man after all.

"And you?" she asks, passing me a menu.

"Thirty-two." Her head bobs in acknowledgment, but I can't get a read on her expression because she's looking down at the menu in her hands. Is she thinking about how I'm twelve years her senior, and have no business wishing she would look back up at me with those gorgeous blue angel eyes?

Christ, I'm pathetic. I scold myself as I unfold my own menu.

"Can I call you Jack?" Her innocent question catches me off guard, conjuring unwanted memories of Amy to the forefront of my mind again. Specifically the way she chased me down the driveway all those years ago, begging me not to leave her behind.

"Jack, please don't go. Jack, Please! Jack!" Her shrill cries still ring in my ears, and I hate myself all over again.

"No." I push the rough syllable out of my mouth, wishing it was as easy to push my feelings away, too.

"Why not?" She sounds curious, and my hands clench into fists beneath the table. Of all the things for this girl to fixate on, why does it have to be *this*?

To my relief, the waitress chooses that exact moment to reappear, saving me from having to form a response.

Smokey

Now that I don't feel quite as threatened by him, I find myself burning with curiosity about my would-be savior. He doesn't seem to enjoy being asked any personal questions, though. I obviously struck a nerve when I asked if I could call him Jack.

Good. The petty part of my brain activates. *If he doesn't want me to pry into his private life, then maybe he shouldn't have made me a part of it.*

Despite the fact that it's early evening, we both order breakfast, and I add a peanut butter milkshake to mine because I deserve a little comfort food at his expense. My mouth waters just thinking about it, but the tense silence continues between us even after the waitress departs with our order. When he begins drumming his fingers absently on the table top, I can't take it anymore, so I try again at deflecting the awkwardness that we're drowning in.

"So..." I stretch the word out between us, determined to learn a little more about my captor beyond the fact that he's practically twice my age. Recognizing that my questions seem to get under his skin is just a bonus. "Where are you from?" I watch his jaw tick before he swallows.

"Texas."

"And you're a trucker?" His gaze swings to me then, a sexy smirk already in place.

"You've got a firm grasp of the obvious, don't you, Liv?"

His eyes brighten with humour, and I realize it's at my expense. Heat rises in my cheeks as I blush involuntarily, and narrow my eyes at him.

"It doesn't hurt to be sure, *Jack*."

My defensive tone and sarcastic nickname erase the laughter from his face, leaving me feeling an odd pang of regret as the light dies in his eyes. But I brush it off. I shouldn't care about his demons when he could potentially become one of mine.

"Where are you headed?" I continue to prod and he lets out an exasperated sigh.

"What is this, twenty questions or something?" He rubs the back of his neck nervously while looking around for the waitress, probably hoping she'll materialize with our food and save him from responding once again.

"Or something," I shoot back, getting annoyed now myself. "Why don't you want to answer my simple questions? It's literally the *least* you can do after putting me here, in this situation... with...you." I don't sound nearly as sure of myself when I finish as I did when I started.

"Okay, look." He turns to me, giving me his undivided attention for the first time since we exchanged names, and I'm taken aback all over again by the soft warmth in his eyes. "I'll admit, I didn't think this thing through, alright? I don't have a tidy, little list of answers to give you. I saw you standing there with your angel eyes, split lip, and all the bruises you can't even begin to hide..." His voice trails off as his eyes rake down my body before he shakes his head as if distracted. Throwing his hands up as if to say, *what else could I do,* he adds, "I couldn't just leave you there after that." Shrugging his shoulders, he lets his hands drop to his lap.

Fresh tears prick at my eyes as I try to process what this man has done for me. He actually *saw me* when no one else could. Or would.

"I'm sorry if the– Hey, whoa, why are you crying?" He becomes visibly rattled by the moisture leaking from me, and I hiccup in watery amusement at the distraught look on his face. "I'm not going to hurt you, Smokey. Tell me you believe that?" He demands as he folds around me in the booth, like he can protect me from the whole world. My breath catches at his proximity, and I wonder at the way it lights me up with anticipation instead of fear. I've never felt this way before. I want to give him what he wants.

"I believe you," I whisper, just before his lips brush mine.

Jackson

I didn't mean to kiss her. In fact, I've been trying to think of almost anything but that ever since I saw her back at the gas station. She's too young for a man like me, and even though I know that, when I saw her crying again I just couldn't stand it. I'd have done anything to dry her tears. Now that I've started, I can't believe I've spent my entire life not kissing her. I don't know how I'll ever be able to stop.

"Sirloin steak, cooked medium rare, scrambled eggs, bacon, hash browns, and a short stack with a side of link sausage, and a peanut butter shake."

I pull away from her suddenly as the waitress deposits our food on the table, and I do my best to ignore the hurt expression that Smokey wears as I scoot away from her, putting precious inches of space between us. "Will there be anything else?" The waitress asks, her impatient demeanor firmly back in place.

"No, thank you, ma'am. This will be all." I offer a tight, polite smile that doesn't reach my eyes, which is just fine, since the small, round woman is already walking away from us.

We eat our food in a silence so thick I could cut it like my steak, while I pretend that I still have control of the situation.

Smokey

I t's been an hour or two since we left the little diner behind, and nobody has said a word since he jumped away from me like my lips were on fire. I have no idea how to navigate this situation, so I'm left at the mercy of following his lead.

As the sun makes its way down the western side of the sky, I lean up to pull the sun visor down, but it doesn't do me any good. I'm too short for it to offer me any type of relief from the way the brightness blinds me.

With a sigh, I flip the visor back up with more force than necessary, feeling Jackson's eyes on me for about the hundredth time since we left. I ignore his searching gaze, and avoid the glaring light coming through the windshield by looking around the cab of the truck.

There's a small cabin area behind our captain's seats that includes a narrow bed along the back, with a mini fridge built into the paneling behind my seat, and a small microwave mounted in the shelf space above it. There are more shelves and little alcoves built into the other side, behind the driver's seat, filled with a few non-perishables and miscellaneous personal items.

I'm trying my best to be aware of everything, but I can't stop thinking about the way it felt when he kissed me. So different from anything I've ever experienced before. It makes me hyper aware of his presence next to me, of every move he makes, but not the way I was of Uncle Mike. This is something completely different. Something I don't know how to name.

I can count on one hand the number of things I know about him, and even then that's only if what he says is true. He claims that he's a trucker from Texas, and I also know that he smokes and that he's been to prison. Some of the tattoos I can see on his hands, arms, and neck have a roughness to them that I recognize as prison ink. Uncle Mike had similar ones, so I became very familiar with how they look.

Oh, and he's twice my age. Can't forget about that, now can we? Especially not since I lied to him about mine. I told him I was three years older than I actually am. Well, more like two years and some change. My eighteenth birthday is just a couple of months away.

Honestly, I don't even know why I lied. I told him my real name, so why did I feel the need to hide my age? I know it doesn't make a difference. It never did to my uncle, or any of his twisted friends.

Don't go there.

So far, Jackson hasn't given me any reason to believe he's anything like my uncle. *Besides taking you.* I argue with myself.

I remember what he said back at the diner, his reasons for doing it. Without thinking, my tongue slips out and traces the split in my bottom lip, feeling the sting, and tasting the faint coppery tang that still lingers there. My eyes drop to my legs and the many bruises that dot them, clearly visible from under the black denim bunched at the creases of my thighs. And then my gaze lands on the little band-aid stuck to my ankle. The one that Jackson put there just a little bit ago before he fed me and gave me his shoes to wear. I can't recall the last time anyone ever showed that type of concern for my well being. The last time someone was that gentle with me was probably before my mom left.

Dad was never the same after that. Once she was gone, it was like nothing mattered anymore. Not even me. He got hooked on drugs, and married his dealer's barely legal sister so that he never had to go without his fix.

Sometimes I wonder if he had known what Uncle Mike would do to me once he was gone, would he have fought harder to stay? Would I have mattered enough for him to want to live to protect me?

Mostly I just fantasize about it being the reason why he killed himself. I get more comfort out of pretending that he felt guilty enough to do *something* for me, even if all he did was leave me alone to rot in the Hell he created.

I sneak a peek at Jackson as he drives. The way he holds the wheel does something to me. It's sure and relaxed at the same time, almost as if the machine he guides is just another extension of himself. He's confident in his ability to control it. As I observe him from under my lashes, it occurs to me that if this man wanted to hurt or incapacitate me in any way, he certainly could, and probably already would have by now.

Could it actually be possible that I'm *safe* with this perfect stranger?

Jackson

She's finally still over in the passenger side, slumped over with her head resting against the window. I can't see her face through her hair, but if I had to hazard a guess, I'd assume she's fallen asleep. It's about time, too. She's been on edge, her eyes bouncing all around the inside of the cab, looking at everything in here but me until they finally drifted shut about an hour ago. Who could blame her? Even in her sleep I can tell that she has no reason to trust me.

Usually I enjoy getting lost in the drive. Lulled by the vibrations and sounds of the road, I know I have complete control behind the wheel. I am the master of *this* universe. This time, though, it's been a chore to keep my eyes off of her and on the road, the pretty, little smoke show.

Hell, It's been a struggle not to want her ever since she walked past me back at that sad, little gas station. As hard as that is for me to admit to myself.

It makes me feel like I'm no better than my piece of shit father. Like the poison apple didn't fall far from the toxic tree. I want so badly to believe that I'm better than him, but when I look at her, I feel possessive and powerless in a way that I don't know how to name. She's just a young, broken stranger to me, after all.

She shifts restlessly against the passenger side door, mumbling something unintelligible as her head slides against the glass.

I probably should have found a place to stop before now, but I didn't really have a plan when I stole her. Once it was done, I figured we better get over the stateline before we stopped for longer than it took to eat a meal and squirt some dirt.

I've been surfing the radio, listening for any indication that she's been reported missing, but I haven't heard anything to be concerned about. And even while that's good for me, because it would be a real pain in the ass to have to dodge law enforcement right now, I find myself fighting to control the rage that wants to boil up inside of me on her behalf.

I glance over at her again, and even in the dark, the paleness of her skin glows like moonlight. It's a stark contrast to the shadows of her bruises.

Returning my eyes to the road, my jaw clenches as my hands tighten around the wheel, the leather squeaking in quiet protest under the intensity of my grip.

It might not have been the right decision. But I'm not sorry I took her.

Smokey

I'm jostled awake as Jackson pulls the big rig off the road and onto the shoulder. Amazed that I drifted off, my gaze shoots to the windows to get a bearing on my surroundings, but it's pitch black beyond the glass. The only things that cut the inky darkness are the headlights in front of us, and the shining stars above.

"I'll be right back." His voice is raspy, and even through the darkness I can feel the warmth of his eyes on me.

"I've got to put some cones out around the truck. For safety." He tacks the last two words on like an afterthought before he goes on. "In the interest of safety, it would also be best if you stayed put. Don't. Run." These last two words he speaks seriously, like they're each their own sentence.

"Who knows how far you could go out here," he continues casually. "And I'll be honest with you, Liv."

I roll my eyes at the stupid name he keeps calling me.

"I won't chase you."

His tone is laced with importance, and my stomach drops at what he's implying. I actually *could* run. I could escape, be free for *real*. But then I'd be taking my chances out *there*. In the dark. I wouldn't get very far wearing his too-big-for-me shoes that offer about as much protection as the flip flops I lost back in the dust. Not to mention my complete and total lack of wilderness skills whatsoever. I'd be lucky if the mosquitos didn't suck me dry before a gator or something eats me alive. Not to mention all the spiders.

I can't fight the shiver of revulsion that wracks my body at that particular thought, and I nod my head to demonstrate that he's made his point. I understand what he's telling me. He stares at me intently a moment longer, the gravity of his gaze settling on me like a warm blanket, and then he's gone, exiting the truck and closing the door.

It isn't until I'm alone inside, that I wonder what we stopped for and why he would need to set out cones. Surely we're not just going to stop *here*. Right?

My eyes zero in on the single twin bed in the sleeper cabin behind the cockpit like area we've been sitting in. I saw it earlier when I was looking around, but I never considered...My thoughts trail off, because that's not entirely true. I *had* considered that something like this might happen. But like an idiot, like a fucking lamb to the damn slaughter, I allowed myself to be stupidly hopeful that he really wasn't like every other man I've ever had the bad luck to encounter. But why would he be any different? Because he was *nice* to me? Am I really so pathetic that that's all it took to get me into a stranger's custody without much of a fight?

I sneer in disgust at myself, half a second away from grabbing the door handle and flying out of the cab after all, when the driver door swings open causing me to jump what feels like a mile out of my seat.

My heart beats wildly in my chest as Jackson's presence fills the space beside me once again. Just like before, I feel like

Bambi frozen in a pair of headlights that are barreling straight towards me, and I'm powerless to stop the inevitable collision. There's no way I could fight him off, if that's the way this goes. I snort out loud, wondering how else it could possibly go.

"What's that about?" His southern drawl shifts my focus from inside my head, to him.

"What's what about?" I ask, confusion evident in my tone.

"The sound you just made. You snorted or something."

My cheeks heat with embarrassment as he calls me out on the sound I just made.

"I was just wondering what we stopped for."

The sentence bursts out of me *Alien* style, and I feel the warmth deepen in my face. Thank goodness it's too dark to see the tomato color in my cheeks.

"It's late, and I'm tired." He says this like it's obvious, before brushing past me into the sleeper cab.

My breathing becomes fast and erratic as I listen to him shuffle around behind me. I refuse to turn around and look. I mean, I don't even *want* to.

Liar, liar, pants on fire.

I taunt myself with a sing-song voice inside my head that I immediately bitch slap back into silence. I don't have to take that kind of shit from *myself*.

It's never been more evident to me than it is right at this moment that I need *so* much therapy.

"Smokey."

The rough quality of his voice saying my name, my *actual* name, instead of calling me Liv, sends a shiver down my spine, just like it did back at the diner. It feels so close and intimate inside the truck all of a sudden. I swallow, and I would swear that he could hear it.

"Yeah?" I finally squeeze out. Where did all the oxygen in here go?

"Come here."

The simple command fills me with a strange mix of fear and longing. I was afraid it's what he was going to say, and yet, I waited with bated breath, almost worried that he *wouldn't* say it.

"Uhmm..." Wait, is that *my* voice? Why does it sound so breathy and needy? "No, thanks." I continue, marveling at my own ability to form coherent words at the moment. "I'm comfortable up here."

"Smokey."

Okay, did his voice just get *deeper*? Goosebumps break out across my skin as I absorb the command in his tone. "I won't say it again."

The gravity in his voice compels me to turn, finally, and face him. It's too dark for me to see him, so I just stare into the shadows as I speak.

"What if I don't want to?" The question comes out like a whisper, even though I tried to keep my voice strong.

"I won't hurt you, little girl." His voice is soft; comforting.

I try not to laugh sourly at his words, feeling like Little Red Riding Hood about to be devoured by The Big Bad Wolf.

"No offense, but I've heard that before." My voice still sounds so small, but I'm proud of myself for keeping it steady and not letting it wobble.

"Let me prove it."

His response is so confident, I almost believe him. Or maybe I just *want* to believe him. To believe *in* him. To believe that someone can actually want me without causing me pain.

"Come lay down with me, Little Smoke Show. Let me hold you."

His voice is gentle instead of commanding this time. Vulnerable. And that nickname: *Little Smoke Show*. It makes my toes curl involuntarily. "It's the only way I can be sure that you'll still be here when I wake up. That this wasn't all some crazy fever dream born from guilt, loneliness, and the absurd Georgia heat."

He whispers into the darkness between us, and maybe I'm crazy, but when he said holding me is the only way he can escape, it unlocked something in me. Something that let him convince me to go to him in the dark, even though he already told me that if I ran he wouldn't chase me.

Jackson

Her tentative touch grazes my naked chest as she searches for me in the darkness. She'd probably be more comfortable if I had left my shirt on, but at least I'm still wearing pants. I usually sleep naked, with a pair of shorts close by so that they're easy to pull on if I need to get up in the middle of the night for anything.

Not giving her any more room to hesitate, I pull her into me so that we both go tumbling down onto the small bed together. She makes a startled squealing noise as she falls against me, and I'm glad she can't see me smile at her distress. I'd hate to ruin all the progress I'm making at gaining her trust.

Lying on my back, I hold her on top of me so that her head rests on my chest, and I can wrap my arms tight around her, keeping her flush against me. If she tries to move, I'll know, and right now, she's trying so hard *not* to move, it's got her uncomfortably stiff in my arms.

"Relax, little girl. I've got you." I whisper to her, stirring the hair on top of her head directly beneath my chin. I feel her chest expand against mine as she draws in a deep breath. When she lets it out, her body melts into mine, and I have to start telling certain parts of my own body to stay relaxed as well.

It takes mere minutes before she's totally limp in my arms, the cadence of her breathing accompanied by her small snores letting me know that she's out like a light. It's been a big day for her. For both of us.

"What the fuck are you doing, Jackson?" I ask the darkness, hoping an answer will magically materialize at the forefront of my mind. Instead, all I get are more images of Amy and everything I left behind. When I finally went back, it was too late. She was already gone.

Is that all I'm doing here? Trying to save Smokey the way I should've saved Amy a decade ago? If so, mission accomplished, right? I've gotten her out of whatever hell hole she was surviving in. I could drop her off anywhere now, and let her make her own way. In fact, that's exactly what I should do. When we hit the road again tomorrow, I'll ask her where she wants to go, and I'll do my best to get her there.

Then we can go our separate ways.

I COME AWAKE EASILY when her body moves on top of mine. My cock, already swollen and stiff thanks to the physiological wonder of morning wood, throbs painfully under her as she wriggles against me some more.

"No, don't. Please! I'll be good, I swear, just let me go!"

The desperate whimpers clear the fog of desire from my mind as I realize that Smokey is thrashing around on top of me, fighting like hell to get loose. Reflexively, I hold her tighter, trying to quell her struggles, but it only serves to increase her efforts. She arches backward suddenly, thrusting her head up and clipping me right in the face as I look down at her.

"Fuck!" The expletive bursts out of me as I immediately let her go to cup my hands around my nose which is already beginning to drip blood down my face and into my beard. Without my arms to stabilize her, she falls to the floor with a thud, and I step over her in the confined space searching for the roll of toilet paper I keep stashed back here. Attempting to unravel the little, white squares without bleeding all over the thin material proves as futile as trying to hold onto the Little Smoke Show a moment ago. With a wad of paper pressed to my face in one hand and the blood-spotted roll in the other, I turn back around to face her and assess the situation.

The pale blue light of the dawn erases the deep purple of night from the sky, allowing me to see that she's still on the floor, sitting with her back against the bed paneling. She's obviously awake now, the fight from before nowhere to be seen in her small, deflated body. Her hair is disheveled, and along with the dirt still staining her tank top from yesterday, there's a fresh spot of red staining the turquoise material near the top of her shoulder. I also can't help but notice the crimson streak that travels down the swell of her breast, before disappearing into her cleavage.

The sight of my blood painted on her body has the desire from earlier roaring back to life, but I do my best to control my very physical reaction by recalling that she was begging to get away from me just a few moments ago. Begging me, or the person from her nightmares, to stop.

It makes me wonder who and what I saved her from. An abusive father, or maybe a violent boyfriend. Perhaps a husband since she's in her early twenties. It doesn't really matter, except that the thought of another man's hands on her, making her cry out in fear and pain has me feeling things I have no right to feel for her. She's a stranger to me, after all.

So then why does it feel like she's mine to protect?

Smokey

I'm beyond embarrassed.

First, I can't believe I actually agreed to sleep with this stranger. Not just any stranger, but a smoking hot ex-con who's almost old enough to be my dad. Who also kidnapped me from the only home I've ever known. If you can call it that.

Second, I can't believe I actually *fell* asleep. How could I have possibly felt safe pinned to his chest under the weight of his heavy arms? Do I have *no* self-preservation skills? I mean seriously.

Third, of fucking course I had a nightmare. Because even if my heart tries to convince me that he feels safe, my unconscious mind still recognizes the danger he represents. And because of that, now he's standing about two feet away from me, with a ball of toilet paper obscuring the bottom right half of his face. *Why do I feel bad about that?*

In the early morning light, my eyes eat up the exposed muscles and dark tattoos that cover his torso, getting lost in the intricate image of Death and his iconic scythe clasping an angel with broken wings plastered across his right side.

It was a shock, but not an unpleasant one, to encounter his firm, warm skin in the dark last night. I couldn't help my sound of surprise when he pulled me forward suddenly, causing me to fall into the wall of his chest. The shocks kept coming when he indeed held me there, on top of his body, enveloped by the scent of tobacco and cedar and sweat, so different from the sour smells that used to suffocate me when Uncle Mike climbed into my bed.

And when he whispered to me that he had me, I just...I don't know. I didn't want to fight anymore. Is that what reassurance feels like? Safety? It feels an awful lot like trust. But that's crazy. Because I don't trust Jackson. I can't. I shouldn't. I won't!

"I'm sorry." I finally croak out, looking down at my shorts as I pick at the frayed hem. My voice cracks, but I don't repeat myself, allowing the broken syllable to hang there in the air.

"You have nothing to apologize for, Smokey. I'm the one who should be sorry." His voice is muffled slightly behind the white mass pressed above his mouth, but his tone is gentle.

"I guess you sort of have a lot to be sorry for." I say, a small smile coming through my tone.

"To be clear," he starts, and his voice has taken on an edge as he lowers the bloody toilet paper from his face. "I'm not sorry I took you. I'm pretty sure my instincts were spot on about you, and you were all but *begging* for a way out of whatever life you were stuck in."

He takes a step closer to me and I gulp, tipping my head back further to keep eye contact with him because looking away now would be impossible.

"I'll *never* be sorry I saved you, Little Smoke Show. I'm only sorry you had to suffer so long before I did."

The way he's looking at me is beyond intense, especially with the smears of blood that still mar his bearded face. My core contracts involuntarily, causing me to clench my thighs together while he continues staring down at me.

He looks feral. Like some sacred warrior who's just sworn himself to protect me at all costs.

And damn if I don't believe him.

Jackson

Neither of us speaks while I finish staunching the flow of blood from my nose. Not until I hear one of the truck doors popping open while my back is turned.

"Smokey–" I move reflexively, reaching toward her.

"I just have to pee," she says hurriedly, waving the discarded roll of toilet paper like a white flag as she slips out of the vehicle.

Through the windows, I watch her disappear into the brush that lines the side of the road, and my heart beats wildly in my chest as I wait for her to reappear from the foliage. What I said last night doesn't seem to matter anymore.

I can feel adrenaline oozing into my limbs, ready to go after her if she doesn't return soon.

This isn't how it's supposed to end, I tell myself, seconds away from hunting her down and hauling her back when I spot the turquoise color of her tank top through the trees. I release a breath, relaxing my shoulders while running both hands through my hair.

"Get a fucking grip, Jackson. It's not like you can keep her."

I say it out loud, hoping to get through to myself, just before the passenger side door opens and she climbs back into the truck. After she declines eating any of the food I have to offer, we hit the road before the sun has fully risen in the sky.

IT'S NEARLY NOON AND I'm still trying to figure out how to start a conversation about how this whole thing should end when Smokey suddenly clears her throat.

"So, I'm going to need some...things," she says without looking at me.

"What do you mean?" I ask, and cut my eyes in her direction just in time to catch her exasperated expression.

"You know. *Things*," she says, putting emphasis on the last word, like that will help me decode whatever the hell she's trying to say.

"Okay," I say, nodding my head without taking my eyes from the road. "Treat me like I'm stupid, and try to be specific."

"Oh, that'll be a stretch," she mouths off under her breath, and I bite my cheek to keep a smile from spreading across my face.

"What was that, Liv?" I ask her, amusement evident in my tone. She sighs as if she's annoyed.

"How about a hairbrush for starters?" She holds up a tangled hunk of curls to make her point, and I toss a smirk in her direction.

"Check out the glove box." She rolls her eyes before leaning forward and doing as she's told.

In the open compartment are some assorted tools, electrical tape, and resting right on top of the thick, worn truck manual is my black hair brush. She snags the latter before flipping the compartment closed again. Already getting to work detangling her thick tresses, she adds, "Okay great, but I'm going to need more than just your hair brush."

Tightening my grip on the wheel, I pray for patience as I try to get a handle on my growing frustration.

"Why don't you just sack up and tell me what you need, Little Smoke Show?"

Her pretty, little mouth pops open in shock for a moment, and that's all it takes for my imagination to run wild. My dick is only too eager to accommodate the direction of my thoughts, and I try nonchalantly to adjust my position in the seat in order to hide my growing erection. I've been popping them like a hormonal fucking teenager ever since I fought her up into my truck. That might play a part in why I'm not sorry I took her, but I won't be telling *her* that.

"I need..." her tentative voice fills the cab again, drawing me out of my less than chivalrous thoughts, "*girl* things." Her cheeks are the most adorable shade of red right now.

"And honestly, a change of clothes would be really nice," she adds quickly, crinkling her nose as she looks down at herself. "I'm starting to smell. Plus, If I had known I wouldn't be going back, I would've worn a different outfit." I look over just in time for our eyes to connect as she lets out a snide little chuckle.

I recognize that getting her a change of clothes could be good for me too, in case anyone reported her missing after last night. She shouldn't be wearing her "Last Seen In..." clothes anymore. And now that she's mentioned it, I don't exactly smell like a basket of roses either. Since we're not in Georgia anymore, it wouldn't hurt to make a brief stop. We can grab a shower, and another bite to eat. Even though I wouldn't normally stop this often for simple creature comforts, I find I actually want her to be comfortable with me.

It occurs to me that once we stop, she might not want to resume this little road trip with me. We've officially crossed the state line into Alabama. I've rescued her from whatever she needed rescuing from. This could very well be the end of our little fucked up journey together. Technically, that would be for the best.

So why does the thought of going our separate ways make me feel so hollow inside?

Smokey

He hasn't said a word since I told him that I have feminine needs. Something I anticipate from the heavy sensitivity in my breasts, and the warning cramps that have already begun to radiate through my lower back.

He looked over at me when I talked about my clothes, and an odd, almost sad expression overtook his features. I'm unsure of what I could have said or done to make him feel some type of way.

Is it because I mentioned my need for tampons? Is he upset, because now that means he can't be sexual with me? Why does that make me feel disappointed? Do I *want* him to be sexual with me? I've been wanted, but I've never wanted anyone *back* before. It never mattered. My uncle always took what he wanted anyway. Sometimes he even let his disgusting, drug-addicted friends have a turn with me.

He would offer me up as a 'good faith gesture' whenever he couldn't cover his debts from using too much of the product he was supposed to be pushing. And if I tried to say no, or fight back? The consequences later never made it worth it. The only time he ever left me alone was when I got my period, though it didn't start out that way...but that's a horror story for another time.

I remember the way Jackson looked this morning with blood in his beard as he told me he wasn't sorry he took me. He looked absolutely savage, and I should have been afraid. But I wasn't. In my mind, the image evolves into one of him on his knees before me, his beard stained red from being buried in my pussy while he licks the blood from his lips and tells me he's not sorry.

I feel my cheeks inflame and slide a surreptitious glance to the left to see if he's paying any attention to me. Thankfully his eyes are on the road, his expression still clouded by his own thoughts.

What the hell is going on with me? It's so unusual for me to have these types of thoughts and feelings.

My head is so full of confusing questions that I don't have the answers to, I don't even notice we've been driving through a small, rural town until he parks beneath the big, yellow sign of a dollar store. There isn't much to see around us, but it's more civilization than I'm used to.

"I haven't heard anything about a missing person that matches your description, so it's probably safe for you to go inside with me and pick out...whatever you need," he says to me, and suddenly his trivial radio scanning makes sense.

I blush when I consider the risk that he took when he stole me off that old, dirt road in Georgia. The risk he's taking now, letting me go into this place, and paying for whatever I select since I don't have a dollar to my name. In fact, I'm completely dependent upon him, otherwise this would be the perfect opportunity to make a getaway. But get away from what? He hasn't hurt me or even tried to touch me beyond the way we slept together last night.

Nerves fizz in my gut like a shaken soda bottle when I recall the soft way he spoke to me, and my subsequent surrender to his wishes. But even then, he didn't try to take advantage of me. If I approached yet another stranger and asked for help, I might not be so lucky.

As long as Jackson is willing to see to my needs without seeming to expect anything in return, my safest bet is sticking with him. I won't examine the twinge of relief I feel at having come to that decision.

While I was sitting lost in thought, Jackson had time to make his way around the large vehicle to meet me at the passenger side again, just like he did yesterday. I try to ignore the butterflies that take flight in my belly when he holds his hand out for me, but they turn into a swarm of hornets when I let his warm, rough palm envelope mine. I don't *think* it's fear, but I can't quite put my finger on the emotion I'm experiencing. The sensation is completely foreign to me.

He helps me down from the truck and then does something entirely unexpected. He lets my hand go. My steps falter for a moment, unsure of how to proceed. Are we not doing things the same way we did at the diner? My cheeks color with embarrassment at having misunderstood the dynamic between us, and I tilt my head downwards to stare at my feet as I resume walking, hurrying to catch up to his long strides.

He's already waiting for me with the door open, and warmth washes over me as I walk past him into the store. I try not to bask in the simplicity of his gesture because human decency shouldn't make me so fucking weak, but here we are. *Sack up, Liv.* I hear Jackson's voice in my head, and smile a little to myself as I hunt down the feminine hygiene products.

SMOKE SHOW: A FORBIDDEN AGE GAP ROMANCE

After picking out a brand of tampons I've only ever seen advertised on TV, I glance around for my escort, trying not to panic when I don't immediately find him in my vicinity. He didn't leave me, did he? He wouldn't.

I have no reason to believe that about him, but I do.

When I finally track him down, he's in the minuscule clothing and shoe section, staring down at the less-than-diverse options the little country store has to offer. Reassurance swamps me when I find him standing with one arm crossed over his chest, supporting the other, as his chin rests in his hand, looking very concerned as he observes the meager selection.

"Looking for something specific?" I quip as I approach, my heart racing for an entirely different reason now.

"You need better shoes," he supplies without looking away from the footwear.

"I do?" I stop to look down and observe my very small feet inside his very large shoes.

"Are you kidding?" He asks, picking up a pair of simple, white canvas sneakers to examine them more closely. "You can't run properly in those things." He tosses a nod toward my feet, but he still doesn't take his eyes from the shoes in his grip.

"Oh," I say dumbly. "I didn't know that was a problem?" He must hear the question in my tone because his gaze shifts to me.

"You could hurt yourself." He says it seriously before returning his focus to the sneakers.

"Right," I say, drawing the word out as if he just spoke nonsense.

"Try these on." He thrusts the shoes suddenly in my direction, showcasing a smattering of random tattoos climbing up his forearm.

"Whatever you say, Jack." I offer him a jaunty salute as I take them from his hand, and I don't miss the way his body tenses as he registers the nickname. I feel instant remorse, but do my best to squash it because kidnappers don't deserve sympathy...Probably. I also want him to tell me why he doesn't like to be called Jack. He keeps calling me *Liv*, so it only seems fair.

The shoes fit like he already knew my size which is both kinda hot and a little creepy at the same time. In an effort to dispel the tension that is always crackling between us, I make a joke questioning his sexual orientation because of his uncanny ability to pick out shoes. To my dismay, he pins me with a flat, icy glare, which is impressive when you take into consideration the naturally warm ocre of his eyes.

"What if I am gay?" The question is cold and hard, like his stare. His stance has shifted, as if he's issuing me a challenge, and my mouth gapes like a fish, as I try to figure out how to pull my poorly clad foot out of it. "I-I didn't think— I didn't mean— I wasn't trying to be—" I sputter, and he lets out a vicious chuckle.

"Don't worry about it, Liv." This time when he uses the annoying name, instead of a casual term of endearment, it sounds like he's spitting it at me. Like he's disgusted, causing the familiar burn of shame to warm my cheeks.

"I'm not gay, Little Smoke Show." He looks me up and down salaciously to punctuate his statement, and for the first time, the predatory look in his eyes sends a shiver of apprehension running down my spine. "Maybe I'll even prove it to you sometime." The quiet words are uttered like a threat before he turns away, releasing me from his intensity.

My whole body sags in relief as he moves away towards the socks hanging on display, taking the shoes he insists I need with him. Anxious to put even more distance between us, I trail further down the aisle as I pick through the cheap clothing, wishing desperately that the floor would open up and swallow me whole.

Jackson

I shouldn't have threatened her. I know her off-hand comment, "You know what they say about a man who knows how to pick out shoes..." was said innocently in jest, but I can't help the way I reacted. And that's definitely what I did. React instead of respond.

Just like I did yesterday at the truck stop when I was caught off guard by the stunning little smoke show.

Gibbs, the leader of the prison ministry, would be so disappointed if he could see how quickly I'm unraveling all the progress he helped me make on my impulse issues. I shake my head as I begin the ritual he taught me of counting down slowly from five, breathing in deep between each number until I feel like I'm in control again.

It's not her fault, I mentally remind myself while reaching for a pack of white cotton socks I don't even really see. She doesn't know me. She doesn't know that I've been to prison, or about any of the things that happened to me there. She doesn't deserve my misplaced anger and annoyance.

I tilt my head to the left to see her examining some clothes a little further down the aisle, the dark curtain of her hair falling over one shoulder and hiding her face. She holds a pair of denim shorts up to the front of her body while turning to look behind herself, trying to see if there's enough material between her fingers to cover her thick, heart-shaped ass.

I find myself sending up an indecent prayer that there's not.

I used to be able to think of a million reasons why I shouldn't touch her, but the longer we're together, the less I can recall what any of those reasons are.

After comparing the first set of shorts to two other sizes, she shrugs her shoulders and selects two pairs in the same dark blue color, before refolding the others and putting them back in their respective spots on the shelf.

Her eyes, made brighter by the blue denim in her hands, flit to mine briefly, catching me watching her. Immediately her face colors, and satisfaction unfurls in my chest while a smile tugs at the corners of my mouth. I fucking love watching those roses bloom in her cheeks. She's the most beautiful creature I've ever seen. She quickly turns away, hiding my flowers from me as she moves to the other side of the aisle to examine the T-shirts and tank-tops.

She listlessly picks at a few before sighing and putting them back. She works her way back down towards me, lost in her examination of the generic summer designs. I blatantly watch her, unashamedly curious to see what else she will pick out. She toys with a gray shirt that proclaims, *I woke up like this*, before her eyes travel upwards a little and light up. Excitedly, she bounces up onto her tiptoes, causing her amazing tits to jiggle and sway as she reaches for a stack of black, athletic tops. Finding her size, she pulls one down, adding it to the shorts she already chose. This time, when her eyes meet mine, there's something in them I've never seen before: a spark of elation.

"I've always wanted one of these fancy, supportive tank tops," she supplies, dropping her embarrassed gaze to the floor as her cheeks burn that delicious shade of red that ignites a fire in my soul.

"Grab another," I tell her without even thinking. I really just want to see her light up again, but she blanches instead.

"No, one should be fine. You're already doing so much for...me..."

Her words trail off as I reach above her and grab one more of the stretchy tops.

"There." I hand it to her, adding it to the small stack she's accumulating in her arms. "Two for two." I smile down at her.

"Thanks." She mumbles to the floor.

"Anything else?" I ask, and watch her eyes flick over to the socks and underwear then back to the floor.

"Uhmm," She starts, but I hold up the pack of socks I already grabbed.

"Already got you covered, Smoke Show."

With a huff, she steps around me and snags a package of panties off the shelf, quickly tucking it out of sight beneath the other items she holds.

"I'm ready now," she says quietly.

I wonder briefly if her cheeks would feel as warm in my palms as they appear before I take stock of everything she's carrying: two pairs of shorts, two tank-tops, a box of tampons, and some underwear. That, coupled with the socks and shoes I picked out for her, still isn't very much when I have a duffel bag full of clothes out in the truck that I stop to wash at laundromats as needed.

"Pick out a few more things, Liv. You're not my prisoner, and there is no dress code." When she ignores me, I stop to place my fingers under her chin and tip her face up so I can snag her gaze. "You deserve to have nice things, Smokey. Things that are *yours*. Unfortunately, all we have at the moment is this." I gesture with my other hand to the store around us while offering what I hope is a comforting smile.

She nods her head as tears turn her eyes into crystals, and my chest constricts with a longing I have no right to feel as I look down at her. She has no idea what she does to me. The effect she has. I clear my throat before looking quickly away.

"I've got a couple of things to grab myself, but I'll meet you at the registers up front in ten. Sound good?"

She sniffles and nods again, looking down at the floor, and for reasons I can't explain, I pull my hat off, readjusting it so that the bill faces backwards before I lean down to kiss the top of her head before walking away.

Smokey

I watch his retreating form disappear around the corner as I try to process what just happened. A girl could get serious whiplash caught between these mood swings. He's all scary and on edge one moment, then he's telling me that I deserve nice things and kissing me the next. I'd be lying, though, if I said it didn't give me the warm fuzzies inside.

Get a grip, Liv.

I try to recall when exactly his became the voice inside my head. I much prefer it over Uncle Mike's.

Remembering that he told me to meet him up front in ten, I turn a quick circle, taking in the rest of the clothing around me. Since I already grabbed some more shorts and tank-tops, I pick out a pair of jeans I hope will fit, along with a couple of random t-shirts. At the last second, I grab a pair of soft, black leggings and an oversized, gray tank I looked at earlier. Jackson is right. I deserve a bit of comfort, the same way I deserved that peanut butter shake back at the diner yesterday.

Feeling like I have more than enough stuff now, I make my way to the front of the store with full arms. Jackson is nowhere to be seen, so I stand awkwardly to the side while I wait for him.

"You next in line?" A petite, blonde woman with a large, drooling baby perched on her narrow hip asks me.

"Sorry, no, not yet. I'm waiting for someone." I look around for the person in question as I scooch out of the way to allow her and her slobbering offspring by me.

I wait so long, I wave two more people ahead of me, as I resist the urge to panic. My eyes dart all over the store, searching for any sign of my... My brain stalls, because what even is Jackson to me? Technically, he's my captor, but he already said that I'm not his prisoner. So, then what exactly am I to him? Thankfully, I'm saved from trying to solve any of these puzzles when he reappears, walking towards me with a small four-pack of toilet paper under one arm, the shoes he picked out for me hanging from his fingertips, and a simple, black backpack slung over his other shoulder.

I can't ignore the relief that pours through me when our eyes meet and he smiles. I hadn't let myself officially form the thought yet, but part of me was scared that he had just left me here. And that's what the sudden kiss to the top of my head was about earlier, like it was some sort of weird goodbye.

"Miss me?" he jokes as he places his items onto the tiny conveyor belt. I roll my eyes in response, unwilling to acknowledge how much I did, in fact, miss him, as I set my own collection of things down on top of his.

"How are ya'll doin today?" the girl behind the counter asks, her big, hazel eyes eating Jackson up like I'm not even here. I clear my throat, being unnecessarily loud, and her gaze flicks to me briefly before she blows an outrageously large, pink bubble with her gum and starts swiping items across the scanner.

"Doing well, just passing through." Jackson supplies with a knowing smile after witnessing the small exchange. The cashier blushes, and I roll my eyes again, this time in disgust.

So far, all the females we've encountered react the same way to him. Granted, that's only been two: the waitress from the little diner yesterday, and now this girl here. *And me.* But still. It's annoying that he has the same effect on all of us. It's so unnecessary.

I get distracted from my jealous thoughts when she reaches into the backpack and begins scanning the rest of Jackson's things. Among the shoes, socks, and toilet paper, I spot a tube of Chapstick, a small bottle of SPF lotion, a pink toothbrush, and most shocking of all, a dress. It looks like one of the maxis I purposely ignored earlier. A dress just doesn't scream *practical* when you've been kidnapped, you know?

It's a bright red color dotted with little, white flowers, a slit up one side, and faux pearl buttons down the front. I shoot a questioning look up to Jackson and catch him already gazing at me.

"I told you." He pierces me with the heat in his eyes, holding me captive in a whole new way. "You deserve nice things," he states gruffly, before looking away to pay the pretty, young cashier.

Turning my gaze back down to the floor, I hope that he doesn't see the tears welling up in my eyes for like the billionth time. He's going to think I'm seriously pathetic if I don't get my emotions in check, for real. It would be so much easier if he wasn't being so damn nice to me, though.

Jackson

I didn't mean to make her cry. Again. Nevertheless, her pretty, blue eyes have been too bright with the sheen of tears ever since we left the dollar store. Every now and then, she sniffles and rubs at the wetness on her cheeks, peeking at me from the corner of her lashes, as if she thinks I haven't noticed.

Of course I have. I'm aware of every move the Little Smoke Show makes. She doesn't take a breath without my brain cataloging the way her chest rises and falls with the action.

It just struck me when we were still back at the store, that even though I took her from everything she knows, left her with nothing, she hasn't asked me for a single thing. Save for a hairbrush, some tampons, and a change of clothes. She barely even begged me to let her go. I wonder if she knows how remarkable that is? *Remarkable or just plain stupid?* My father's voice chimes from the darkest corners of my mind, prompting me to employ my patented countdown technique until he's just the way I like him: Gone. Banished.

That man was dead to me before I ever killed him.

Smokey isn't stupid, and she deserves so much more than the bare minimum. I don't think she's aware of that, though. I don't know why I felt inclined to try and give it to her, but it is what it is. Besides, it's no big deal. It's not like I got her very much stuff.

Everyone needs a toothbrush. Especially since I don't relish the idea of sharing my own. The SPF lotion is because I still don't know how she survived in The South with that creamy, fair skin, and I'd hate to see it burned. The Aquaphor lip balm is for the split in her lip, and the dress I saw earlier, while I was in the clothing aisle with Smokey.

As she walked by the small selection of summer dresses, bypassing them all completely, flashes of that picnic scene from *Armageddon* went through my mind, and I just couldn't help myself. I had to double-back and grab it.

Of course, in my fantasy, it wasn't Ben Affleck and Liv Tyler I saw. It was me and the beautiful Little Smoke Show, wearing the dress I bought for her, as we lay in the sun-dappled grass while I explored the peaks and valleys of her stunning little body with a box of animal crackers. *My own little Liv.*

My imagination ran wild for a moment, right there in the store, before I was able to reel my thoughts back in.

Juggling all the miscellaneous items I picked up made me recall the way she was carrying all her clothes in her arms, so I made sure to grab something small and convenient to store it all in, hence the backpack. It's not very large or flashy; just a black canvas bag with a small pocket on the front. Something that can be *hers*.

It was more than I had intended to spend at the little, country store, but not enough to really affect my finances. It's pretty easy to put money away when you live like I do: On the road, alone, only buying necessities and amenities as needed.

Being in prison taught me that I don't need much. And being a felon on the outside has taught me that the world isn't very accepting or believing in the rehabilitation system. Once you have a record, you *always* have a record. People treat you like you aren't a human being capable of growth or change. You're forever a danger to society, no matter what you were in for. That's why the isolated life of a truck driver is perfect for me.

All I have to do is get online and check the load-boards for available jobs, call on what I want, and if no one else has already taken it, Black Betty and I head to wherever the load site is.

I've been very careful with my cell phone usage in front of Smokey, though. So far, she hasn't seen it or asked about a phone at all. I'm guessing whoever she's justified in running from never let her have any access to one. It makes sense. Why would an abuser give his victim any means to call for help, stop him, or get away? I know I wouldn't. *You haven't*, I remind myself, but I push that thought away as I pull the rig into a *Love's Travel Stop*.

"I've got to run in and pay real quick, but you can wait here."

She nods without looking at me, but she doesn't appear to be crying anymore, at least. Without saying anything else, I get out of the truck and head inside to pay for a tank of diesel fuel and a shower. I don't acknowledge the intense urge to turn around and make sure she's still sitting right where I left her.

WE'RE BARELY OUTSIDE of Heflin, Alabama, your typical, small, southern town, surrounded by larger, metropolitan areas. I'm trying to keep us out of heavily populated places as much as possible. Both because I don't want to overwhelm her with the culture shock, and because I'm not ready to expose her to so many ways she could get away from me. Right now, she's dependent on me for everything, and I like it that way.

Are you even any better than whoever you saved her from? The thought crosses my mind as I finish filling the gas tank, and I shove it away resentfully. Of course I'm fucking better than whatever waste of fucking space was harming her before. I may have hurt and scared her, but there's a difference between harm and hurt. Harm implies an ongoing condition that stays with you. Hurt is something you can heal from. *She'll be able to heal from me.*

Why does that thought unexpectedly sting?

"Grab your stuff and let's go," I tell her gruffly when I open my door and climb back up to grab my own bag out of the back.

"What? What for? Where are we going? Are you getting rid of me?" Her voice rises in panic with each question, and I feel my lips curve into an unstoppable smile.

"What's the matter, Smoke Show? You gonna miss me?"

"No!" She answers too quickly, then blushes so prettily for me. "I mean, of *course* not! Are you kidding?!" She rolls her eyes. "I'm just curious," she tacks on at the end.

"Uh-huh," I say, the smile still tugging at the corners of my mouth. "Come on, Liv, you're finally getting a shower." I tell her in answer to her rapid-fire questions.

"Really?!" She all but shrieks in her excitement. "Why didn't you say that sooner?!" She swipes her new black bag from the floorboard at her feet and slides out of the truck before I can even finish exiting the vehicle myself.

Smokey

I'm practically vibrating with excitement. I get to take a shower. A real shower, with heat and water pressure and everything. A shower that Uncle Mike won't be able to interrupt and make himself a part of.

An uncontrollable shiver rolls through me at that particular thought. I can't remember the last time I had complete and perfect privacy. I'm not sure I ever really have. Jackson is like my own personal fairy godmother right now.

I bounce from foot to foot impatiently as he consults his receipt, punching a code into a little, high-tech keypad lock on the thick door. Once open, he holds it for me to enter. Walking past him to set my new bag on the countertop under the mirror, I watch his reflection follow me inside and close the door. Apprehension dances down my spine, and I spin around quickly, grabbing the bag back up, holding it in front of my body like a shield.

"What are you doing?" I can hear the shocked surprise in my tone. He looks around the brown tiled room as if it should be obvious.

"I told you already." He hangs his bag from a hook mounted on the wall. "We're going to shower."

"Nooo…" I draw the syllable out between us nervously. "You said that *I* was going to shower." He sighs, dropping his head to stare at the tiles beneath his feet for a moment like he's trying to gather his patience.

"Liv, we both need one. I realize that you'd be more comfortable by yourself, but *I'm* not comfortable leaving you alone, okay?"

Despite feeling like he dangled a carrot in front of my face, only to yank it away at the last possible second, I find his admission surprising and more comforting than it should be.

"You can go first," he goes on, oblivious to the confusing emotional turmoil he causes within me, "and I'll wait over here by the sink brushing my teeth or whatever, until you're finished. Then we'll trade places." He turns abruptly toward the sink in question then, dismissing me like a child. *You are a child compared to him*, I remind myself.

There's no way he won't see the scars now.

I shove the thought away, and with suddenly trembling fingers, I hang my bag from another mounted hook over by the shower stall. I unzip it shakily, taking stock of all the new things he got for me.

"Uhmm…" I start, my voice small and hesitant. I try not to let it shake like my hands. "I don't have anything to wash with. Or a towel." I'm not facing him, but in lieu of a response, I hear him rummage around through his things, and feel the heat of him at my back when he approaches me from behind.

"Here." Looking down to my right, his big hand offers a brick of brown soap that seems like a reasonable size until I take it from him and hold it in my own tiny palm. Immediately following the abnormally large cleansing bar, he passes me a black loofah and a white bottle of two-in-one shampoo and conditioner.

"Thanks." I barely even breathe the word as I take the items from his hands, still not willing to meet his eyes.

"Hey." He catches me by the arm before I proceed into the shower alcove. My eyes jerk to his, startled and afraid, but he doesn't let me go. "I won't hurt you, Smokey. I promise." He sounds so sincere as his thumb gently traces over the skin on the inside of my wrist. Inexplicably trusting in his words, I ease myself out of his grip with a shy nod before disappearing behind the lip of wall that offers the shower a scant bit of privacy.

Once hidden from view, I take a deep, shuddering breath while tears fill my eyes. *You're okay, Smokey, just keep breathing. In through your nose, and out through your mouth. In... And out... In... And out...* I school myself into getting my nerves under control.

Moving slowly and methodically, I remove my clothes, tossing them over to where I left my bag hanging outside the stall, so they won't get wet. My eyes dart all around the opening to my right, looking for any sign of Jackson being less than honorable, even though I can hear him splashing over by the sink like he said he would be. Self-consciously clutching an arm up to my chest to hide my breasts, I reach out with the other to start the shower and squeal when I'm immediately blasted with icy cold water.

"Is everything alright?" I hear the urgency in his tone and what sounds like footsteps shuffling towards the enclosed space.

"I'm fine! I'm fine! I'm fine! Don't come over here!!!" I shout, borderline hysterically. "It was just really cold, and I wasn't prepared," I tack on in a rush, praying that he'll listen and won't feel the need to investigate further.

Oddly, I almost want him to see me, to see heat mingle with desire in his gaze...but I know the permanent evidence of my shame would probably kill any budding attraction growing between us.

No one is ever gonna want a girl as used up as you, anyhow. The intrusive thought is unwelcome, but it succeeds in bringing me back to the here and now.

With the water now warm, I soap up the loofah Jackson gave me to use. The suds smell amazing: like spicy autumn leaves mixed with whiskey, and a touch of campfire smoke. It smells like him, I realize, and smile a little to myself as I rub the rich lather onto my skin. The loofah scrubs over me in such a delicious way, a sigh of pleasure escapes my throat, and my eyelids drift closed, savoring the extraordinary sensation. I've never experienced such luxury before. It's almost enough to make me forget that a stranger stands only a few feet away from me while I'm exposed and vulnerable, save for the fact that his very masculine scent permeates the steamy air around me.

With my eyes closed, I allow myself to pretend my scars disappear. That there's nothing marring the view of my nakedness in front of Jackson. In the safety of my mind, I present to him my smooth, supple, untouched flesh, and watch his warm brown eyes darken with appreciation. In my fantasy, no one has ruined me yet, and I choose him to be my first...maybe my only, since it's make-believe after all.

I move the loofah lower, rubbing down my stomach, ignoring the ridges of scar tissue I meet there. I continue down my thighs and in between them while fantasy Jackson tracks every move I make with his hungry, predatory gaze.

When I rub the abrasive material behind me, soaping up my ass cheeks, I pretend I have a perfect, unblemished complexion, from my head to my toes. I picture myself with a body worthy of the gaze of a man like Jackson.

When I hear the sound of something clattering from beyond the shower opening, my eyes snap open and the fantasy bleeds away, like water down the drain.

After casting a nervous glance towards the opening to check for Peeping Toms, I pick up the shampoo and conditioner duo and squeeze a large, white dollop into my palm. There's no special, seductive scent to this one, just a generic *clean* smell, and I don't waste any time rubbing the viscous mixture into my scalp.

I stand under the spray for a few moments, letting the bubbles pop in my hair while I enjoy the hot jets of water running over me, easing muscles that have been tense for what feels like my whole life. It's not until I've rinsed and turned off the water that I remember he never gave me a towel.

"Uhmm, Jackson?" I'm back to awkwardly trying to cover my chest with one arm, while the other extends down my front to cover my pussy.

"Yeah, Liv?" His voice is rough, though he answers immediately.

"I still need a towel."

Suddenly, his big hand appears holding a fluffy, gray towel for me to take.

I snatch it eagerly from his fingers, rushing to squeeze the excess water from my hair a little before getting the material wrapped around my body. Heaven forbid he actually see the nightmare of my nakedness.

Only once I'm fully covered do I emerge from the shower stall, a small "Thank you" leaving my lips as I walk past him to the sink. It's easy to avoid his reflection in the steam-covered mirror as I pick up the comb he has laid out and begin working it through the wet, tangled mass that occupies the top of my head. He brings my bag over from the shower, fishing out the SPF lotion he bought for me along the way.

"Make sure to use this all over." He sets the bottle on the edge of the sink before turning and disappearing behind the dividing wall.

Aye, aye, Captain, I want to snark, but I manage to keep my smart mouth shut this time. His clothes fly out a moment later, his belt buckle clanking loudly against the tile where they land.

"I won't take as long as you did, so don't waste any time getting that lotion on and getting dressed." He tosses out before the water starts, cutting off any attempt at a response I could have made. I roll my eyes at his commands as I finish combing out my hair, but I don't take any chances by disobeying.

I hurry through plaiting my hair into a thick braid that falls over one shoulder and brushing my teeth with his toothpaste before rubbing in the lotion just like he ordered. I tell myself it's because I wanted the luxury of it though, and not because he told me to. I'm pulling on the soft, black leggings and gray tank top by the time the water shuts off.

"Hey, Liv? A little help here?" He calls for me, and even though it's not even my name, I find myself stupidly responding.

"What do you need?"

"The towel?" He says it like he can't believe I'm this dense. Snatching the soggy cloth up from the edge of the counter where I left it in a ball, I shake it out a little before holding it out for him to grab. As I do, I notice the red streak across the center of it and recall the warning cramps I've been experiencing all day. Heat floods my face as he takes it from me, and like word-vomit I can't help but blurt out, "I'm so sorry, Jackson!"

"What? Why?" Concern laces his tone, and a moment later, he steps out where I can see him. My brain momentarily short-circuits as I take in his glistening chest and dripping abs, the towel slung low around his waist showcasing the deep-cut "V" of his hips.

"There's stain," I say, pointing like a moron. "I mean *a* stain." I correct myself. "On your towel. From me." I babble on like an idiot, my face as red as the offensive streak. He looks down in what feels like slow motion to inspect the souvenir I left behind, and I know the moment he understands what he's looking at, because his whole body suddenly goes rigid.

Oh my God, Lord Almighty, please just smite me where I stand. This cannot be happening.

I stand frozen, caught between the past and the present, waiting for the wolf to finally take off the sheep's clothing and show me how angry and feral he really is underneath. I wait for him to tell me that if he wanted me to bleed for him, then he would have *made* me, and that what I left on his towel is dirty and disgusting, just like Uncle Mike taught me.

But none of those things happen.

When he looks back up at me, his nostrils are flared and his pupils are so big and dark I think they must be dilated.

"You have nothing to be sorry for." His voice is deep and guttural as he pins me in place with his stare. "This," he points to the towel, gesturing to the stain, but doesn't take his eyes off mine, "is completely natural, and it's a sign your reproductive system is working exactly like it's supposed to. The only thing it should stop for is when–" He stops suddenly and closes his eyes, breathing deep. He swallows, and I'm mesmerized by the way his Adam's apple works in his throat. "The only reason your cycle should stop is if you get pregnant." He clears his throat as he turns away, retrieving something from his bag and then disappearing into the shower stall again. I mean, I don't need him to tell me how *my* body works, but now I can't stop thinking about making a baby with him, and more than just my face feels hot from the thought.

He comes back out a few seconds later wearing a pair of black jeans, the towel slung carelessly over his shoulders. He doesn't spare me a glance, thank goodness, because I can't stop eating him with my eyes. His tattoos are dark and evocative, all done in varying shades of black, with little pops of red here and there. Red for blood, I notice with a gulp as he walks straight to his bag, tucking both soaps and the loofah out of sight in their respective places before grabbing a corner of the towel and rubbing vigorously at his wet hair. Discarding the wet cloth, he pulls out a folded, white t-shirt, shaking it out before pulling it on. He stands in front of me fully clothed, still wearing his shower shoes, and somehow, he still manages to look like some sort of fabled Viking warrior.

"Ready to go?" he asks, snatching up his things from around the sink to pack them away with everything else before sitting down on the toilet situated by the sink to exchange his wet shoes for his boots.

"Uhmm, actually I..." I trail off, unsure of how to tell him that I need to use the very appliance he's currently sitting on. In fact, I probably need to change out of these leggings that I've no doubt already ruined. My cheeks heat for what feels like the billionth time.

"Just spit it out, Liv," he says with a sigh, and fed up with his pushy, cavalier attitude while I try to navigate the roller coaster of my emotions during a high-stress situation that *he* created, I do.

"I need some fucking privacy to put a tampon in, okay?! I'm standing here, bleeding into my leggings right after getting blood on your towel, and I can't even have the fucking *space* to be embarrassed, or change, or clean myself up, or *anything*!" I'm shouting by the time I finish, and Jackson looks at me like I'm a crazy person. Maybe I am.

"I'm sorry, Smokey." He sounds sincere and a little confused. "I just wanted to demonstrate that you can trust me."

"You want me to trust you?!" The words are still exploding from my mouth. "Try demonstrating that *you* trust *me*, and stop treating me like *I'm* the one who's been to prison!"

He pulls back suddenly like I just slapped him, and his jaw ticks before he responds.

"Once a criminal, always a criminal, is that how it is?" he asks defensively.

"Well, you kidnapped me, so what does that tell you?" I snarl back bravely before I can stop myself.

"You don't think a man can change? Be better than he was?" His tone has calmed, but his eyes still condemn me as I try not to laugh hysterically at his words.

"Not in my experience." I shake my head, feeling defeated as I lower my gaze.

"Maybe the issue here is with your lack of experience, then."

His carefully spoken words slice at my already fragile self-esteem before he quietly exits the bathroom, leaving me alone to wonder why the space I fought so hard for suddenly feels so empty.

Jackson

Back at the truck, I pace back and forth in agitation as I wait for Smokey to join me. The cigarette I lit to calm myself doing nothing to soothe the sting of her words. She's not wrong, and that's what really gets under my skin. I have been to prison, and I did act like a common criminal when I took her. What did I expect? To be her hero? This isn't a fucking fairy tale. The truth is, I'm just a stranger to her. Just because she feels like mine, doesn't mean she is.

The way I want to object to that last thought tells me I'd do well to remember it.

If space is what she wants, then space is what she'll get. It's better if I keep my distance from the tempting little smoke show anyway. I can't keep dragging this out. It's not good for either of us. I need to find out where she wants to go and get her there. End of story.

All of those thoughts, including my resolve, go up in flames when, through the thin haze of cigarette smoke, I see her walking towards me in the dress I picked out for her.

Everything around me grows fuzzy as my attention centers on the little devil approaching me. The dress fits her tight little body perfectly, showing off every delectable curve. Including the rounded pooch of her lower belly that she keeps smoothing her hands over as if she's self-conscious of it.

The scar tissue I spied there in a less-than-honorable moment of weakness while she showered doesn't change the way I want her. Not by a long shot. They just remind me to be gentle with her, something I failed to remember when she was losing control back there.

If I'm being honest with myself, the marks I saw on her body, coupled with the abject fear in her eyes when she apologized for the blood on my towel might've played a part in the white, hot rage that overtook me back there. I just don't understand how someone could attempt to destroy something so perfect. It's like scribbling on the *Mona Lisa*.

When she's close enough to hear it, I let a whistle out in appreciation of her appearance, and am rewarded when a nice, peachy blush stains her beautiful cheeks. It makes me wonder if her ass would bloom the same beautiful shade of red under my palm, and instantly, I have to turn and nonchalantly adjust my growing erection, tucking it into the waistband of my jeans.

"I'm not wearing this for you," she informs me as she draws closer, my new favorite color still staining her face and neck. "I just don't have anything else that's loose and non-constricting, and I don't think I deserve to be in even more discomfort than I already am."

I grit my teeth and swallow the sharp, defensive remark that wants to jump off my tongue.

"You look good, all the same," I say instead, as we both climb back up into the truck and get situated in an awkward silence.

"Thank you." Her voice is so quiet that if I hadn't been staring indecently at her mouth, I probably wouldn't have heard her at all.

"You're welcome."

With the air between us crackling with tension yet again, I sigh as I start up the truck and ease us back out onto the road.

"HOW LONG DO YOU THINK you'll be giving me the silent treatment, Liv?"

A noncommittal shrug of her shoulders is all I get in response to my question. We've been driving through Alabama for a little while now, and other than picking up an old, black Sharpie from the dash and asking if she could use it, she hasn't spoken a word or even looked my way.

After agreeing to her request, I watched in fascination as she turned the white canvas shoes I bought for her into a sketch pad. A riot of realistic-looking vines and flowers fills the empty white space of one shoe, while she works meticulously to fill the other. Occasionally, her brow furrows, and her pretty, pink tongue will poke between her teeth in the most endearing look of concentration I've ever seen. I could probably go on watching her just exist next to me forever, and that, more than anything, is what finally has me doing what I should have done yesterday.

"Is there somewhere I can...take you?" I glance at her, feeling suddenly unsure. "Somewhere specific you'd like to go?"

For the first time in hours, her hand stops moving, and she sits completely still beside me.

"Do you want to get rid of me?" She answers my question with one of her own, and I can hear the uncertainty in her voice even though she still won't look at me.

"Of course not!" The answer is out of my mouth before I even have time to think about it, and I realize in that moment how true it is. I *don't* want to get rid of her. Even though I know I *should*. "But I'm headed back to Texas to pick up another load..." I add, looking over again as her hand resumes its steady movement, drawing over the canvas of her shoe.

"Where are we now?" she asks, still without looking up.

"We're about to cross over the Mississippi state line. We'll be rolling into Louisiana probably sometime tomorrow," I supply, and she finally looks up, gracing me with her beautiful, blue gaze.

"That's where *The Big Easy* is, right?" she asks innocently.

"New Orleans?" I ask for clarification.

"Yeah." She nods noncommittally as she resumes her decorative task.

"Yeah, that's in Louisiana. Is that where you want to go?"

She nods her head again, her tongue peaking out between her teeth as she focuses on her art.

"Can I ask why?" I inquire, both to keep the conversation going and to satisfy the burning curiosity in my chest.

"Just something my dad used to say about my mom before he died." Her tone is distracted as she answers. I tighten my hands around the wheel, annoyed by how little attention she's paying to me. I mean the *topic*. She's being so vague with every answer, not giving any little piece of herself away.

"So I didn't save you from a shitty father, then," my reply is sharpened by my desperation to know more about her. "How about your mom?" She caps the marker with a sigh, like she's frustrated that I keep ruining her concentration.

"Actually, I had the shittiest of fathers," she supplies matter-of-factly, and it takes all I have not to correct her. Pretty sure my old man takes the cake on that one, but she starts talking again so I push him from my mind and give her my undivided attention.

"My mom left when I was just a baby, and he used to get so high, going on and on about how she was big and easy, so it made sense for her to go back there." Smokey shrugs her shoulders. "I don't want to be like her but..." She pauses, leaving me dangling on the thread of her story.

"But?" I prompt her to go on when she doesn't automatically continue.

"But if she could start over there, then maybe I can too."

She looks out the window when she finally answers, her tone suggesting she'd be more than happy to end the conversation. But I just can't help myself. Now that I've got her talking, I don't want her to stop. I want her to tell me everything.

"Who gave you that, then?" I gesture to her face and the healing split in her bottom lip. I'm momentarily enthralled when she traces the wound with her tongue, and I have to force my eyes back to the road so I don't accidentally kill us both.

"Why do you care?" she shoots back, her annoyance at being interrogated beginning to show. "It's over, you saved me, the end. I don't want to think about it anymore." She crosses her arms over her chest defensively as if she's trying to create a physical barrier between us, and I allow her to drop the subject.

In an effort to ease the hostility that keeps building between us, I ask a different question.

"How did you know I've been to prison?"

She's silent for so long I don't think she's going to answer.

"Your tattoos," she finally says, causing me to glance down at my hands, flexing them on the wheel as I try to observe them from her perspective. I'm wondering how she's so familiar with prison ink when she asks, "Do you want to tell me what you were in for? Maybe it will make us both feel better."

Her tone is both disinterested and hopeful, and in the spirit of trust, I realize I can't ask her about her story when I'm unwilling to share mine.

"I'd have to go back to the very beginning for it all to make sense," I tell her.

"So?" she asks sarcastically, motioning to herself strapped into the passenger seat. "Where else am I going to go?"

Casting a small, sad smile in her direction, I begin.

"I was just sixteen when I lit out from home like the Devil himself was chasing me. I guess maybe he was." I feel my mouth twist into a parody of a smile. "My momma died giving birth to my little sister, Amy, when I was just four years old, and Daddy was a mean son of a bitch who liked to rule me with his fists. But by then, I had had enough of being his punching bag." I glance at her, trying to convey through my expression that I know exactly what it's like growing up in Hell, because I did too.

"I waited until he passed out, drunk off his ass and worn out from wailing on me, like always, but the beatings didn't seem to hurt as bad that day. I guess because I had already decided they would be my last.

Once I was sure he was out for the night, snoring like a chainsaw, I scraped myself up and high-tailed it out of there like my ass was on fire. Taking nothing but a loaf of bread and a jar of peanut butter, I hopped on my bike, and pedaled like hell into the dark. It didn't matter where I went, as long as I got away."

I stop to shake my head at the memory, a massive lump forming in my throat like it always does when I remember the way my twelve-year-old sister ran after me in her pink pajamas, begging me not to leave her behind. My voice is thick with emotion when I manage to speak again.

"Now, Amy had just turned twelve that year, but our dad had never taken to hurting her before. Not once. In fact, I would have said he doted on her. She was daddy's little girl." My voice is full of pain when I look at her again, seeking absolution I don't deserve. "How could I know that once I was gone, he'd turn on her? How could I know that he would do so much more than just beat on her like he did me? His own daughter!?" My tone is laced with anguish as I force the words out.

Smokey doesn't say anything. Instead, she gently reaches her small hand across the space between us to rest it on my forearm, silently reassuring me that I'm not back there, reliving the worst time of my life. I'm here, in the present, sitting next to her, the warmth of her touch giving me the strength to continue my tale.

"When I finally went back for her..." I stop again, unable to speak about the tragic, unnecessary death of my little sister. The way she killed herself because our father, a man who should have been responsible and dependable—a man who was supposed to be *safe*—got her pregnant. If I say it out loud, I think I'll be sick.

"Oh, Jackson, it wasn't your fault." She tries to placate me, but the sympathy in her eyes is too much to bear.

"Wasn't it, though?" I ask incredulously, tears I've tried so hard to suppress for so long running freely down my face. "If I would have just stayed there and taken my beatings, the sick bastard never would have knocked her up, and she'd be here now!"

I swallow the bile rising in my throat while her delicate fingers fly to her face in an attempt to cover a shocked gasp.

"Jackson, I'm so sorry," she says gently, "but don't you see?" She continues to try and console me. "He could've kept beating you until you were dead, and then it wouldn't have made any difference. You would still have been gone, either way. And you don't know that he wouldn't have turned his attention to her as she grew up anyway..."

"No!" I cut off the words I don't want to hear her say. "I would have been there to stop it! I should have been."

A thick and heavy silence descends between us for a moment. Smokey doesn't push me to continue. She just sits quietly with me in my shame, her small hand still resting on my arm, a connection that gives me more comfort than I care to admit. Only when I feel like my emotions are back in check does she gently prompt me to continue.

"So what happened next?"

"I killed the mother fucker," I say flatly. "When he told me that Amy ended her own life just two years later– two years after I had deserted her– I wrapped my hands around his throat and I didn't let go until I ended his."

I look over to gauge her reaction to me admitting I murdered my own father, and am a bit surprised, and not a little relieved, to find her able to meet my gaze without flinching.

"Good," she says evenly with a hard glint in her eye. Then she says something completely unexpected. "I'm proud of you."

I look at her completely dumbfounded before replacing my eyes on the road.

"What? Why? How could you possibly be proud of what I've done?"

"Because you went back for her, Jackson. Because you loved her, and you wanted to make it right, even if you couldn't." A single tear rolls down her cheek before dripping off her chin to disappear into the fabric of her dress. "That's all I've ever wanted."

Something shifts inside me. Something I'm not sure will ever be the same again.

In a bid to escape the fire ants that are suddenly crawling under my skin, I pull off the road into the first place with a parking lot big enough for Black Betty to fit in. To my relief, it looks like a little country dive bar.

The Good Lord must be looking out for me, because I could abso-fucking-lutely use a drink right about now.

Smokey

We pull off the road suddenly, bouncing into a small clearing in front of what appears to be a dirty shack on stilts with a rickety porch that looks like it might collapse if the wind blows too hard. A large, moldy piece of plywood leans against the ribbed, steel siding with the words, "Muddy Joe's," spray-painted in bold, black letters with an arrow pointing towards the door. In the window is an orange neon sign boasting 'Live Bait' right next to a duct-taped piece of cardboard that reads, "The best fried catfish this side of the Mississippi!"

"Are you alright?" I ask, eyeing all three signs dubiously as he puts the truck in park.

"Yeah, I'm just peachy, Liv," he snaps, and I feel my cheeks heat with sudden, inexplicable remorse. He sighs, dropping his head forward and pinching the bridge of his nose between his thumb and index finger.

"I'm sorry. You didn't deserve that. I'm just...it's hard to talk about the past, you know?"

"Oh, is it?" I say, injecting my tone with exaggerated sweetness when he looks back over at me. "And here I was just having a ball answering all those personal questions you kept throwing at me earlier." I raise an eyebrow at him in playful reproach. His face softens as he cracks a smile, and I don't even have to think about smiling back. I just do.

"You hungry?"

"Not hungry enough to eat here!" I respond quickly, but then my stomach growls loud enough to make me a liar. There's only so much chips and jerky a girl can snack on, and I've reached my limit. He laughs out loud, and my heart leaps at the sound.

"Your stomach sure sounds hungry enough to eat here." He's still smiling, his dimple winking at me through his beard as my face warms with embarrassment...and something else.

"Come on, Liv. Dives like this have a bad reputation, that's all. Kind of like ex-cons." He looks at me earnestly, the meaning of his words not lost on me. "If you gave it half a chance, you might just find you like its rough edges."

The space between us feels charged all of a sudden. Like invisible electricity is arcing between us, throwing sparks that are destined to start a fire.

"Are we still talking about Muddy Joe's?" My voice is a husky whisper, and I can feel myself being pulled towards him like a magnet, leaning in without any conscious thought to do so. And then my stomach growls loudly in protest again, and his eyes light up with mirth.

"Of course we are, Smoke Show. What else?" He's nothing *but* smiles now, the lightning storm between us fading as quickly as it started. "Come on, let's go. Before your stomach really starts to make a fuss." He shakes his head in amusement as we climb out of the truck.

I do my best to smile back, but it feels brittle on my face as I try to puzzle out what just happened...and why I feel disappointed by what *didn't*.

TURNS OUT, ALL MUDDY Joe's has to offer is live bait, as advertised, along with some mix and match fishing gear to go alongside the fried fish being served. Not to mention an award-winning Mississippi mud pie. I know it seems dubious in a place like this, but I'm currently indulging in the latter, while Jackson shovels an absurd amount of catfish into his mouth before washing it down with a swallow of cold beer.

"You gotta try this, Smokey," he says right before packing his mouth full again. "You don't know what you're missing."

"I have to try it before you eat it all, you mean?" I say with an eye roll, plucking one of the greasy pieces from the basket in the middle of our table.

"Oh my God." My eyes close in ecstasy as the flavors roll over my tongue. Breaded and deep-fried with Cajun spices, the fish is crispy-crunchy on the outside while being succulent and juicy on the inside. It's spicy, and buttery, and definitely way better than I was anticipating.

"Joe sure knows his way around the kitchen."

"I told you," he says, reaching across the table to dip his spoon into the decadent chocolate dessert in front of me.

"Mmmmm," he hums in appreciation, and my mouth goes dry as the sound tugs unexpectedly at my core. I clamor for my own beer in self-defense, gulping down the bitter liquid in an attempt to drown the wet heat coalescing between my thighs.

The distraction works, as I immediately wonder if people actually like beer, or if they're all just pretending.

I don't usually drink alcohol, having witnessed firsthand the monster it can turn someone into. And also because of my age, of course. But Jackson thinks I'm twenty, and didn't think twice about ordering me my own beer. Thankfully, this isn't the type of establishment to care about checking ID, not that it would make a difference since I don't have one. He really has no idea just how dependent upon him I really am, and I shudder to think about what I'll do when he leaves me behind. Because it's inevitable...isn't it?

"Okay, Little Smoke Show. Tit for tat. I told you my story, now you tell me yours." His words bring me back to the here and now, where he wipes his hands on a paper napkin before taking another long pull of his beer.

Taking another bite, I chew slowly, inspecting the grease spots on the checkered red and white paper lining the food basket between us, but it doesn't take long for me to finish and swallow. Desperate to keep stalling, I reach again for my own beverage, and this time, I tip the bottle back and drain its contents. Like magic, our waiter, a big, black man with a shiny bald head who introduced himself as Joe, as in *the* Joe of Muddy Joe's, materializes with a fresh round. I smile gratefully at him as I reach for the brand new frosty brown bottle. As my hand closes around the neck of it, the condensation slick against my overheated palm, I can't help remembering the way a six-pack of similar brown bottles felt like an anchor tethering me to another life less than two whole days ago.

"Come on now, Liv." Jackson rolls his eyes in annoyance, tapping his fingers impatiently on the table top. Ignoring him, I empty my bottle for the second time.

It's not so bad when it's cold, I guess. Sucking in a deep breath, I carefully place the glass bottle back on the table and close my eyes. I need a moment to let the liquid courage seep into my veins.

"Are you ready now?" He asks as soon as I blink my eyes open.

Feeling warm and tingly all over, I let go of a sigh and nod my head as I relax, folding my arms together on the table top and leaning forward.

"I told you already that my mom left when I was just a baby. I never knew her. I also told you that my dad died. When I was six."

"I'm sorry," he interjects.

"Don't be." I shake off his sympathy. "He wasn't anything special. Just a parasite. I suspect that's why she left. She didn't want to be stuck supporting him and his habit forever. I guess she didn't want to be stuck supporting me either." I add with a shrug. "Honestly, I don't really blame her. They were never married, and I'd have run too. If I could have." I meet his eyes for a moment, but I'm unprepared for the empathy I find in them, so I dart my gaze immediately elsewhere.

"So yeah, when my dad did finally manage to get married, it was to Kelly." I roll my eyes when I refer to my pitiful excuse for a step-mother. "She was his drug dealer's little sister, and barely even legal at the time. That's how we ended up in The Peach Pit." I refer to the trailer park I grew up in while snagging another piece of fish from the basket. "So that he would never have to go without his *real* love," I say, popping the morsel into my mouth.

"Which was?" he asks, eyebrows raised.

"Heroine," I supply matter-of-factly once I've swallowed. "It was a real *Cinderella*-type of story at first," I go on, staring at my hands as I wipe them with my own paper napkin. "As long as I stayed quiet and kept things clean, I was relatively safe. Until my dad took his own life at the end of a needle. That's when my step-monster got really into slapping me around, and blaming me for his death." Jackson's fists clench on the table and I feel a modicum of comfort that he would feel upset on my behalf.

"She used to say that if he hadn't been shackled with such a stupid, useless kid, then they could have run away together and had a better life." I laugh, but it's a bitter sound. "My father couldn't even be bothered to create a better life for himself, let alone me." I shake my head. "I think she really believed it, though." I shrug my shoulders again as I stare into the past. "Maybe she just needed something *good* to believe in. Even if it wasn't real."

I look down at the table, spinning the empty glass bottle anxiously between my fingers, needing a moment to get my emotions in check. Jackson stays quiet, giving me the time and mental space to sort through my thoughts before I continue sharing them.

"I think she felt saved by him or something. Because as long as my father was alive, Uncle Mike..." My voice trembles involuntarily when I speak his name, and I have to stop to swallow the bile that rises whenever I think of him. "Uncle Mike didn't hurt her anymore." I rush to finish the sentence.

It's a surreal feeling telling him about my life. Right here, right now, sitting across from him with my muscles loose and warm from the alcohol, it feels like it could have all happened to someone else entirely. If only I didn't have so much of the ugly, physical evidence carved into my flesh. Maybe then I could forget.

"Did he hurt you instead?"

His quiet question uttered from across the table pulls me back to the present and compels my tearful gaze to meet his intense one. Unable to form words around the boulder sitting in my throat, I give a quick, sharp nod of my head before looking away again, a single tear escaping my control to run down the side of my face. I don't want to see the disgust when he realizes that I was my uncle's whore.

"He was so nice to me at first, while my dad was still alive," I finally choke out. I need Jackson to understand that I was so confused, and in the end, never had a choice.

"He was the only one who ever paid any attention to me. The only one who could *see* me, even through the haze of drugs." I sniffle at the memories, understanding now that he only saw me then because he's a predator who noticed how easily he made me feel special in a world I was so obviously unwanted in.

"When my dad died..." I pause, steeling myself to say the bastard's name again. "When he died, Uncle Mike was there to *comfort* me." I spit the word 'comfort' as if it's the most revolting word in the English language. Because the things he did to me and made me do were *not* comfortable. It took a long time for me to come to terms with that.

"He crawled into my bed one night while I was crying myself to sleep. He told me it was all going to be okay because he would be my daddy now, and daddy would always take care of me...as long as...as long as..." I begin to tremble, so I close my hands into fists, pressing the crescents of my nails into the skin of my palms. The sting helps ground me back in the moment. "...As long as I took care of him!" I choke on the words, losing my battle with the tears as they fall unchecked down my cheeks. "That was when I finally understood how alone I was...how alone I had always been." I trail off brokenly as despair swallows me whole.

Jackson

I don't say anything as she speaks. I sit still and quiet, telling myself to breathe deep and stay calm until her words halt, her emotions obviously getting the best of her. Everything she's been brave enough to divulge is sickening, and I still don't even know how she got the ridges of scar tissue I spied on her lower abdomen before.

As much as I want to know... I'm not sure I have it in me to make her tell me. I don't think I can ask her to relive what that must have been like. I'm not sure I want to know. Clenching my jaw so hard I fear it may crack, I stay silent and raise my hand to the owner behind the bar in the universal sign for another round.

As soon as the new drinks appear, she looks to me gratefully, immediately reaching for hers and gulping it down with a desperation I know all too well. As I reach for my own, I can only hope the cool liquid will somehow douse the inferno of rage building within me. My memories of Amy are like a tinderbox in my head, and Smokey's words are like a match, igniting them and setting them ablaze, so that the image of my innocent little sister blends with the beautifully broken girl in front of me.

If I close my eyes, I can see them both chasing after me, like colored overlays, begging me not to go... Snapping my eyes open, the surreal moment wafts away like smoke.

With both our bottles empty yet again, our gazes reconnect, and I notice that hers is glassy and her pupils are slightly dilated. I make a mental note to cut her off and make sure she only gets water for the rest of the night.

"I have to pee," she announces suddenly before standing up from the table. "Whoa..." She wobbles briefly before placing one hand back down on the flat surface for balance, the other going to her head as if she's trying to hold it still while the room tilts and spins. I've been there before, too. Never after just three beers, though. It seems my Little Smoke Show is a little lightweight.

"Maybe I should walk you–"

"No!" She cuts me off, standing up straight. I can practically see her fighting against the effects of the alcohol in her system.

"No, I'm fine, I just..." Her brow furrows as she looks around the rustic establishment. "I need to know where to go."

"Right over there." I point behind her to a wood-burned sign that reads *Outhouse*, hanging above a dark, slender hallway. Without another word, she turns and makes her way towards it, only stumbling once before she disappears into the shadows.

As she goes, I can't help but notice the way the guy eating alone a few tables down watches her as she walks by. His eyes linger on her perfect, heart-shaped ass as it sways passed, and I have to stop myself from cracking my knuckles and acting like a complete caveman, pounding my chest and claiming what's mine for everyone here to see.

But she isn't mine, I reluctantly remind myself. She can't be. After everything she's been through, there's no way she'd want *any* man, least of all one like me.

Looking down at my hands on the table, I study them, remembering how she told me she recognized the rough quality of the work as prison ink. It doesn't take a fucking genius to figure out why she knows that, now that she's told me some of her story.

I clench the offending appendages as I look back up, eagerly awaiting her reappearance from the dingy little hallway. The longer she's away from me, out of sight, the tighter my skin feels. I'm about to get up and go find her myself when she emerges, and my chest expands with a relieved breath.

My relief is short-lived when the man who ogled her ass earlier, kicks his thick leg out into the aisle, almost tripping her and stopping her progress back to our table. Back to me.

"Why don't chu sit chur purty ass down here with me, sugar," he twangs drunkenly at her, patting his flabby lap with greasy hands. My girl doesn't offer him a response, acting like he doesn't exist as she goes to step around his leg in her path. But he doesn't let her.

"I said sit chur ass right here!" he spits, his hand reaching out faster than I thought the old drunk was capable of, circling her forearm and forcibly pulling her body down into his. Smokey whimpers at the contact in what could be pain or fear, most likely both, and suddenly I'm there, ramming my fist into the bastard's face without ever telling myself to move.

I grab onto my girl as the low-life's head snaps back, his arms going limp around her as his chair topples backwards from the force of the hit. His legs meet the table, and I hear the musical tinkle of breaking glass while plastic cutlery skids across the floor.

"Hey!" Joe shouts as he lumbers out from behind the bar, anger and concern at war in his tone.

"Time to go, Liv!" I hold my hand out to her, gratified when her little fingers wrap tightly around mine, and we book it out of Muddy Joe's together.

Smokey

My heart gallops in my chest as we speed out of the parking lot, the back end fishtailing a bit, throwing gravel, before the big tires gain traction and grab the road. We leave the little dive bar behind in the gathering dusk, and even though I anticipate it, no one chases after us.

Settling back into my seat, I look over at Jackson. The knuckles on his right hand, the one holding the wheel with utter control and confidence, are split and bleeding, the sight causing me to feel short of breath for a whole new reason.

He's bleeding again. Bleeding for *me*.

I clench my thighs and bite my lip, fantasizing about what he would do if I were to boldly lean forward and lap at the crimson liquid oozing from his torn knuckles. Just as I'm imagining cleaning the split skin with my tongue, the warm, coppery tang bursting over my taste buds, his gaze clashes with mine.

"Don't look at me like that, Little Smoke Show, or I'll have to pull over and teach you how a man is supposed to treat a woman when she looks like that." His voice is deep and full of grit, and the meaning of his words has goosebumps breaking out all over my body.

I clench my thighs together again as an involuntary whimper escapes me. I've never felt this fever before. My core throbs, craving a release I've never experienced. My eyes flick back to his face when he growls beside me. He actually growls. Like a fucking animal. And I gasp as I clench my thighs even tighter, chasing the wild throb of pleasure that rebounds through me when I release the pressure.

I'm thrown around in my seat a little as he stomps on the brakes, swerving the big rig to the side of the road, bumping into the weeds that meet the shoulder. I don't know how many miles he's put between us and the little bar we just ran out of, but we couldn't have gone far.

That hardly matters as he's hauling me into the back of the truck.

He lowers me to the small bed as the sun sets the sky on fire with burning pinks and oranges. It's a magnificent view, but the beauty of the moment causes sudden anxiety to flood my nervous system, and I place a defensive hand on his chest as he leans over me.

"Jackson I– erm– what about safety?" I flounder for an excuse to stall. I want this, I'm just... It feels like my first time. In a way, it kind of is. It's my first time that *means* something. My first time to choose. But what will he say when he sees my scars? There's no way he'll want me after that. He has no idea how ruined I really am.

"Relax, Smoke Show. I just want to taste." His tone is gentle, but I feel the furnace of embarrassment warming my cheeks anyway.

"No, I..." I falter as I push him away again before covering my burning face with my hands. "That's not what I meant!" There's a beat of silence before he responds.

"What did you mean, then?" The confusion is evident in his tone.

"The cones." My voice is muffled behind my palms. "The ones you always set out for when we stop on the side of the road like this." I finally lower my hands and steel myself to meet his perplexed expression, "for safety?"

I know he thinks I must have been referring to a condom, but I'm not worried about getting pregnant. Uncle Mike made sure that could never happen. Remembering what Jackson told me of his little sister reminds me to be grateful, though, even as my heart aches for what I've lost.

"I'll have you know that those are for legitimate road safety, and I have the permits to prove it." He speaks seriously, almost like he's scolding me, as he moves to sit on the edge of the mattress. His shoulders sag as he lets go of a great sigh.

"If you don't want to do this, Smokey, all you have to do is say so." He looks down at me earnestly as the sunset makes campfires out of his warm, brown eyes. "I'll never force you to do anything you don't want to do."

"Except for when you kidnapped me, and when you made me share a shower with you." My voice is small, but my tone is light and a little teasing. He laughs bitterly before hanging his head down for a brief moment.

"Yeah, Smoke Show. Except for those times." When he looks over at me, the sincerity in his gaze lights up the butterflies in my stomach, turning them into lightning bugs inside me. "I'd like to think that I've done a lot to show you that you can trust me, though. To let you know I don't want to hurt you, and that you're safe with me."

I let his soft declarations settle over me, processing his words before forming a response. I need him to understand that I want this. Him. I just... I feel suddenly inept and out of my depth. I'm afraid. I might not be a virgin, but I've also never been a willing participant in what we're about to do. What if I don't do it...well? What if I'm not any good at all?

"I do feel safe with you, Jackson." I sit up beside him, reflecting on the truth I just spoke. When he doesn't say anything right away, I tentatively slide my fingers against his until we're holding hands while we sit together on the edge of the bed, watching what's left of the sun go down.

"I've never felt that before," I whisper into the gathering darkness.

Emboldened by the lack of light and the way he makes me feel, I lean further into his warm, solid frame, relieved that he doesn't pull away from me. This whole moment feels so fragile; I don't think I could handle his rejection. "I wonder what else you can make me feel that I've never felt before." I breathe the words into his ear, and before I can blink, he has me on my back with my hands above my head, pinned beneath him once more.

Jackson

"I want you to feel safe, Little Smoke Show, but if you keep playing with fire, you're going to wind up burned." I rasp into the column of her delicate throat as I trace it with the tip of my nose. I can feel her pulse fluttering there, and when I inhale, I smell myself on her skin, the scent of my body wash still lingering from our shower earlier in the day. My cock fills with steel, hardening with the need to claim her from the inside out.

"I need you to tell me you're sure about this, because I don't want you to hate me," I admit before lifting my head from the delectable curve of her neck so I can look into her big, blue eyes. "Come on, Liv, use your words," I urge, watching her expression closely, but she squeezes her eyes closed, shutting me out.

"Don't call me Liv!" The statement bursts out of her as if she's been holding it in for a little while. Taking a steadying breath, she continues, "At least not now. Not during this." When she opens them to meet my gaze, she adds, "I'm sure, but I want to be myself while I experience this...with you."

Her tentative words cause a massive knot to form in my throat, so I nod once to demonstrate my understanding.

"I don't want you to hate me, either," she whispers brokenly into the dark.

"Never," I declare before sweeping my tongue over her plump bottom lip and sucking it into my mouth. She tastes like sin and sweetness, and I devour her with my kiss until we're forced to come up for air. Her pupils are dilated with desire, and she looks beautifully disheveled before me. I don't think I felt this much pressure to do a good job my first fucking time, but I really want to make this pleasurable for her. It's literally the least I can do for the privilege to touch her after everything she's been through.

Taking my time so I can appreciate the sensation of her smooth skin sliding beneath my palms, I run my hands up the back of her legs, hiking her dress up as I go. She leans back on her elbows, her chest rising and falling with shallow breaths as she watches me with equally hungry and frightened eyes.

I wish I could say that her fear didn't sharpen my need for her, but we're all just animals at our core, aren't we? I am a predator, and she is my prey.

"I want to taste you," I tell her, pleased when I hear, as well as feel, her breathing hitch with uncertainty and desire.

"But I'm–"

"I don't care," I interrupt her as I cut my eyes down to the triangle of polka-dotted cotton hiding her exquisite cunt from my view.

"Lift your ass," I tell her, placing my hands on her hips to grip the fabric of her underwear on either side. She hesitates for a moment, and I wonder if she's worried about her scars, but then she does as I say, pushing her feet into the mattress and lifting her bottom up, allowing me to slide the material down over the ample curve of her buttocks.

Sliding the panties free of her legs, I press them immediately to my nose and inhale. I hear her shocked gasp, but my eyes are closed after involuntarily rolling back into my head at the scent of her arousal. I want to drown in it. And that's exactly what I intend to do.

Feeling feral, I press my face into her wet flesh, causing her hips to buck in surprise. I grip them in my hands a second time, this time firm enough to hold her still as I swirl my tongue through her folds. When I locate what I'm seeking, my eyes search for hers, and find them wide with bewilderment as she watches me.

Slowly, I retreat from her pussy, the string to her tampon clamped firmly between my teeth. Her mouth goes slack, forming a perfect "O" as we watch the saturated cotton slip from her body, her sheath gaping briefly as the object slides free. My painfully erect cock leaks copious amounts of pre-cum into my pants, eager to let me know just what I can fill that tight, little hole with, but not yet. I'm only just getting started.

Letting the tampon fall forgotten to the mattress, I position myself more comfortably between her thighs.

"I'm going to worship you, Smokey" I tell her, placing a gentle kiss on her pubic bone. I hear her breath catch one last time, and then I'm feasting on her with a reverence I've only ever felt while praying.

Smokey

Is this real life? Surely it's not. It can't be. Men don't pull women's sanitary products out with their teeth. It isn't right. It's vile, wicked, and unclean. Isn't it? Except that the way he's looking at my pussy doesn't look like disgust. It looks like...awe.

"I'm going to worship you, Smokey," he declares, and the way he says my name... there's a desperate quality to his voice, almost like it's a plea. Then he kisses my skin softly, like an offering. Like I'll be saving *him* by letting him do this, not the other way around.

I don't have time to convince my brain to work properly before his mouth is on me again, eating me with conviction and stealing my ability to form rational thoughts. I can only feel. I *am* sensation. And, God help me, I never want it to stop.

Jackson

She's incredibly responsive under my tongue. Moaning and writhing through my oral appreciation, gripping my head with her thighs, as her fingers cling to my hair in a death grip.

I wouldn't unseal my mouth from her holy fountain if she begged me to. Not now that I know how freely it flows for me.

Her essence is sweet and tangy with a metallic edge to it, but the flavor of her blood is hardly a deterrent. My time in prison gave me a whole new appreciation for female anatomy; how soft they are, and how good they smell. If I'm being honest with myself, there's no part of this woman that I don't want to devour. I want her blood, sweat, tears, and cum to cover me, marking and claiming me the way I want to own her in return.

"J-Jackson, wait!" Her erratic plea is at odds with the way she pushes my face deeper into her magnificent cunt as she rocks her hips, rubbing her sensitive clit against my tongue. "No! It's too much! I can't! I'm gonna...I'm gonna...Ahhhhhhh!!!"

The strangled cry leaving her lips is accompanied by a gush of fluid against my chin that soaks my beard. As her orgasm ebbs, and her moans become quiet, little whimpers, I dip my head lower, so that I can lap up my girl's delicious cherry cream. Her legs tremble on either side of me, aftershocks still pulsing through her as I lick every crease and crevice, sucking her delicate folds clean, reveling in every dreamy sigh that falls from her mouth.

"That was...I've never...I'm so sorry!" she chokes out before bursting into tears. My dick is hard enough to cut diamonds right now, but this unexpected outburst demands my immediate attention.

"Smokey, what's wrong? I didn't hurt you, did I?" I ask, my voice full of concern as I gently brush a few strands of her dark, tangled hair away from her beautiful face. She flinches away from my touch, struggling to push her dress back down as she curls into the fetal position. It's almost as if she's trying to make herself smaller; like she's trying to disappear inside herself.

"Smokey..." I flounder for words as I run suddenly restless fingers through my hair in agitation, wondering how the hell we got here, and how I can make this right. One minute she's coming all over my face and it's utter fucking bliss for both of us, and the next, she's cutting me wide open as she cringes away from me in the darkness.

Am I completely crazy to be losing my head over this girl? This Liv Tyler look-alike who has as much baggage as me? Possibly more. But maybe that's exactly what makes us so good together. Her jagged, broken pieces line up so well against mine.

Smokey

What the actual fuck just happened???

I've had sex more times than I can count, thanks to my twisted uncle and his sick friends, but I've never in my life experienced anything like what just occurred between Jackson and me.

It felt unreal. Like I wasn't in control of my own body, he was. But in a *good* way. Not like how Uncle Mike used to try to control me. He only ever brought me pain and suffering. What Jackson just did felt...*divine*. At least it did until I finally got up the nerve to open my eyes and look at him.

Illuminated by the pale light of the moon, I could make out the dark blood smeared across his face, as if I had conjured him right out of my forbidden fantasy from the other day. In the face of reality, though, I buckle beneath the weight of my shame.

I'm dirty and unclean. All women are. Especially during their monthly trauma.

When I got my first period at fourteen, Uncle Mike went berserk. I can still remember the hate in his eyes when he came to my bed and found me curled up in pain from the cramps radiating through me. I didn't even know what was happening to me, and was just as aghast as my uncle when he parted my legs like usual, not at all concerned with my discomfort, and we discovered together the puddle of blood congealing there. I had hoped that God had finally answered my prayers and maybe I would be allowed to die. Of course, I had no such luck.

I recall the way my uncle hauled me from the soiled bedding, ranting and raving about how I was contaminated, and like God did for our sins, he was going to wash me clean. He threw me into the bathtub, turning the water on as hot as it would go until it was steaming and scalding my tender flesh. He proceeded to hold me down as he shoved a bar of soap inside of me, clamping his unforgiving hand over my vaginal opening to keep my body from expelling the unwanted, foreign object. It burned so badly...But not as much as the old, rusty pocket knife he tried to use to cut the evil from my body when it happened again the following month. I'm lucky he botched it, though I'll bear the scars from that particular attack for the rest of my life.

"Smokey, what's wrong? I didn't hurt you, did I?" The uncertainty tinged with a hint of regret in his voice causes a sob to escape me as I withdraw from his gentle touch. Swamped with guilt, I draw in tighter on myself, wishing more than anything that I could spontaneously combust and become like my name, nothing more than smoke.

How do I even begin to explain that he did the opposite of hurting me? That he makes me feel so safe, and so protected, that my entire system is constantly short-circuiting because I've never been put in a situation where I've been cared for without some kind of string attached.

No one has ever made me feel the way that he does. Like I'm more than damaged goods. Like I'm cherished. Like I'm something worth keeping. And I'm not so sure I'm safe with him anymore, when I'm in constant danger of losing my heart to a man who can't possibly want to keep the emotionally fractured girl he stole from the side of a highway.

Jackson

The last time I felt this fucking clueless was right after killing my old man. Once the rage faded and I was left with nothing but the stark reality of what I had done, I didn't know what the fuck to do with myself. Remembering Amy as she was before I left her behind, I felt no remorse for what I had done. But I didn't feel relieved or vindicated like I had hoped, either. Amy was still gone, and I was still alone. Nothing made that more obvious than the bastard's stinking corpse.

It didn't take much deliberation for me to decide to take responsibility for what I had done, so I drove to the local police station and calmly turned myself in. There was nothing else to live for, and all running away had done was get my sister killed. It was time to stop.

I lucked out with a public defender who wasn't half-bad, and was only convicted of manslaughter instead of murder. Even though I don't regret it one bit, I didn't go back home with the premeditated intent to kill my father. It just happened. Maybe not in self-defense, but finding out about Amy's death pulled a trigger in me, and after hearing about the abuse I endured growing up, and the circumstances surrounding her suicide, it was easily ruled a crime of passion.

SMOKE SHOW: A FORBIDDEN AGE GAP ROMANCE

The first year of my sentence was the worst. I was in and out of the infirmary, fighting off the unwanted advances of other inmates, until one day there was a gang of them that caught me off guard—too many of them for me to handle at once. "Pretty Fish" is what they called me, taunting me with it as they held me down and took turns.

I just wanted to die after that. But I wasn't brave enough to do what Amy did.

Too much of a coward to commit suicide like my sister, I became careless with my safety. Putting myself in any position to get hurt, hoping God would take it all out of my hands, and end my sentence early. That's when Gibbs found me.

We were in the infirmary at the same time, albeit for vastly different reasons. I think he could sense my hopelessness because he just got up out of his bed one day, laid his hands on me and started praying. I tried to brush him off at first, but something about the words he spoke, or maybe it was the way he spoke them, reached inside of my chest and squeezed my heart until my eyes were leaking.

Gibbs didn't just save my immortal soul that day, but probably my life as well.

When I left the infirmary that last time, it was under the protection of The Disciples: the Christian gang that leads the prison ministry on Sundays. Maybe the words "Christian" and "Gang" together in a sentence sounds like an oxymoron, but it's a different kind of social climate behind those bars, and unless you've experienced it, you can never understand. It's survival of the fittest in the rawest of terms.

The Disciples try not to lead with violence, but they also don't shy away from a fight. I learned quickly that a Disciple could give as good as they got, but they were always willing to forgive and forget. Gibbs taught me that forgiveness is of the utmost importance because if we can't learn to forgive our enemies, we won't ever be able to forgive ourselves.

I guess I'm still working on that.

As my faith grew, doing time got a little easier. I actually began participating in the group therapy program, also thanks to Gibbs, and managed to parole out early for good behavior. Unfortunately, being good on the inside doesn't matter to anyone on the outside.

Finding a decent job became a pipe dream with a stint of hard time on my record. I worked one shitty job after another until I had enough money saved up to pay for the course to get my CDL. Sitting behind the wheel of a truck is one of the only places I've found solace since my release. I wish I could say I found it in a church or something, but it is what it is.

I spent a couple years driving for someone else until I could afford to buy Black Betty, and she's been my best girl ever since. Most people don't treat truckers much better than ex-cons, but if I'm going to be treated like shit either way, I'd much rather work for myself than some random dick head who thinks he's got something to prove.

Observing the hotel in front of me, I put the truck in park. When Smokey started crying and went unresponsive, I tried to clean the crime scene off my face before throwing in the towel and deciding we could both use a night out of the truck. Space might be the best thing I can give her right now, whether I like it or not.

I had to drive a little further than I wanted to find the Holiday Inn, but there was no way I was taking her to the run-down Motel Six fifty or so miles back. She might actually want, no, *need*, her own room tonight. Away from me. And there's no way in hell I was going to leave her alone in a place like that.

As much as it pains me, and I'd be a fucking liar if I tried to say it didn't, this might be the last time I see her. I know she said she wanted to go to New Orleans, but after what happened between us tonight, she might be ready to jump ship.

I stare at her sleeping form in the back. She finally cried herself out about twenty minutes ago. She never tried to communicate with me, but I still couldn't bring myself to turn on the radio and drown out the soft sounds of her distress. I listened to every choked sob and gasped breath, attempting to punish myself for letting things get so far out of my control. But just like when I killed my old man, I can't bring myself to regret my actions. If this really is the last time we're together, I'll never be sorry that I got to taste her before she's gone.

Smokey

"Smokey. Smokeyyy..." A soft voice nags at my subconscious, but it sounds murky, like I'm far away or underwater. I haven't slept this soundly since I can't remember when, and all I want is to dive deeper into the void and be left alone. Maybe I can finally catch up on all the sleep I've been deprived of my whole life.

"Come on, pretty, little Smoke Show. It's time to wake up."

It's the nickname that does it.

Reality comes flooding back to me, and my eyes snap open to find Jackson sitting on the edge of the bed, one hand raised above my face as if he's just about to touch me. He halts the motion when my eyes collide with his. In the muted light, his are more than dark, but I'm not afraid of him anymore. I don't think I ever really was, to begin with. I was just...overwhelmed. He makes me feel so much. And I'm not sure if it's right to feel any of it. I have no experience with this, and it leaves me confused and completely at his mercy.

After a moment with his hand suspended between us, he lets it fall to his lap without completing its journey. Not for the first time, I wonder at the way my heart sinks at the lack of physical contact.

"I got you a room," he says flatly.

"You got *us* a room, you mean." My voice is hoarse when I correct him, sitting up from the fetal position I fell asleep in, but my eyebrows draw together when he shakes his head no.

"I mean, yes, I got us both rooms here, but not together." He answers the silent question on my face, and it feels like a punch to the gut.

"Why?" I force the word out, and it's weak and squeaky on account of the sudden lack of oxygen in my lungs. It's a stupid question, I know, but I can't seem to stop the panic rising in my throat. "Don't send me away. Please." I rush the words out before he can even respond. "I don't want to be alone."

I don't care how desperate and pathetic I sound. I finally feel safe in the presence of someone else. Not just safe, but wanted. Protected. I'm nowhere near ready to give that feeling up.

Jackson

"Don't send me away. Please." She begs unnecessarily, pulling at the invisible threads she's already wrapped around my heart. "I don't want to be alone."

Fuck, her desperation claws at me in a way that it shouldn't after only two days of being with her. Less than an hour ago, she was inconsolable because I touched her. Or so I thought. I guess I'm not the only one causing emotional whiplash on this roller coaster ride.

"Okay." I nod, my voice raspier than usual when I answer the plea in her eyes. The way she visibly relaxes at my acceptance has me feeling some type of way. I don't even care that I already paid for the other room even though the front desk clerk informed me that all bookings after ten P.M. are non-refundable. I'd say yes to just about anything as long as it makes her look at me like that.

"Jesus!" she shrieks at me as we enter the lobby, causing the clerk from earlier to jump and look up guiltily from his phone in alarm. "Did you book our rooms like that?" Her eyes are wide with shock as she regards me. The man behind the counter simply rolls his eyes at the interruption, dismissing us and returning his gaze to the device in his hands.

"Like what?" I counter as we step into the elevator together.

"Nothing." She looks away quickly, gazing down at the floor, but not before I catch the way her throat works as she swallows.

When I manage to tear my own gaze away from her, I'm met with my own reflection in the shiny, metal doors in front of me. Streaks of dark red mar the skin of my cheeks, staining my beard as if I had been shoving my face into a jar of strawberry jam, Winnie the Pooh style. The corners of my mouth turn up into a wicked smile, unashamed of the way I ate her like she was my last meal.

At least now I know why the desk clerk kept giving me the side-eye when I first came in to get our rooms. It'll be a damn shame to wash it off.

Smokey

He slides the key card into the electric slot on the door, and I watch in fascination as the locking mechanism whirs, a little light below the handle blinking from red to green. He pushes the door wide, allowing me to enter the room first.

I walk down the short hallway, glancing into the standard bathroom as I pass by the open door. There is only one bed, but I expected that. He got us separate rooms, after all. Or tried to, anyway.

It's hard for me to explain, but the thought of being away from him fills me with pure, unadulterated terror. I've never actually been on my own before, or been with anyone who has taken such good care of me, and I'm reluctant to let that end.

The color scheme of the comforter is warm and modern with soft browns, dreamy blues, and pops of olive green and rusty orange. Across from the bed, lining the opposite wall is a modest little dining table with two wooden chairs, and a narrow chest of drawers with a decent sized flat screen. I'm impressed by the minimal style and luxury of the simple room, but I don't really know if I should be. I don't have any other hotel experience to compare this one to. It's certainly the cleanest and most comfortable place I've ever been in.

124

I'm having so many *firsts* with Jackson. Things that other people wouldn't even think twice about like: owning my own backpack, or picking out clothes, or not being afraid all of the time...It makes me wonder if that has anything to do with the intense connection that seems to be building between us so swiftly.

I tell him that he can have the shower first, even though my thighs are slick with blood and other fluids. Neither of us really cleaned up after what happened in his truck earlier, as evidenced by the crime scene on his face, and I never did anything to stop my flow afterwards, either. I've no doubt ruined the pretty dress he bought me, the same way I did my brand-new comfy leggings.

"No, it's fine. You go ahead," he insists, waving me off as he throws himself onto the queen-sized mattress and plucks the TV remote from the nightstand by the window.

"You don't want to wash all that off?" I blurt out with no self-control whatsoever. Seeing the evidence of what we did all over his face is becoming too much for me. My eyes keep bouncing around the room, looking at everything but him until he's suddenly standing right in front of me, unavoidable, barely a breath of space between us. I didn't even see him move, but now I can't look away if I tried.

"Never." He declares seriously, holding me captive with the intensity of his gaze while the rogue heartbeat in my pussy throbs. "I love the way your blood marks me, Smoke Show" he claims, igniting the ever present embers in my cheeks, "and I'm going to wear your war paint proudly. Without shame..." His warm breath ghosts across my lips as his hands cup my face.

"...For as long as I can." I gaze up at him in wonder just before his mouth covers mine.

Instead of uncertainty, I meet his fervor with my own. Curling my fingers into his shirt, I lick hungrily at the seam of his lips, tasting the coppery tang of myself on them until they part on a husky groan, allowing our tongues to meet in an erotic dance that only makes me crave him more.

I press myself further against him until I can feel the hardness of his erection pressing into my belly. Gone is any hint of fear or mistrust. In their place, I feel only pure need and an odd sense of power unfurling within me.

"Let me taste you," I gasp, turning my head and breaking the spine tingling kiss. Our chests rise and fall in tandem as we both struggle to catch our breath. "Please," I beg, lowering myself to my knees in front of him, desperate to show my appreciation for all he's done...desperate to please him. It's the only way I know how to atone for pushing him away before. "You did it for me, now let me do it for you." I maintain eye contact with him as I boldly move my hands to his waist and start to work on the silver button there.

His big hands envelope mine, halting their progress as he speaks.

"Smokey, wait. I don't expect anything from you. You don't have to do this."

Looking up at him, I search his eyes carefully for the rejection I'm so certain is coming, but that's not what I find. Instead, I'm met with a keen desperation to be trusted, reflected in his dark, sincere gaze, and it speaks to the lonely brokenness that echoes inside the cavern of my soul.

"I know." I reassure him, my voice surprisingly steady. "But for the first time, I actually *want* to." I flick my eyes down to where he's still visibly hard in front of my face before meeting his eyes again. "Please." I repeat, licking my lips in preparation for what I'm asking. "Let me show you."

He squeezes his eyes shut as if in pain, but he doesn't say anything else as I watch his Adam's apple bob up and down in his throat before finally releasing my hands. They waste no time resuming their task, and a sharp sigh escapes his lips as the teeth of the zipper separate to reveal his thick, veiny cock. It springs forward eagerly, as if it's trying to leap down my throat, and I marvel at the bruised color of the tip, and the clear liquid beading there.

Stroking my hand down the shaft causes a whispered, "*Fuuuck*," to slip from Jackson's lips as more fluid leaks from the purplish head. Giving in to my curiosity, I lean forward and swirl my tongue through the salty stickiness accumulating there.

His skin is hot and velvety under my tongue, and I lap at the head of his cock again, acquainting myself with the unique flavor and texture of him.

"Jesus, Smokey," he grits out. "Your mouth feels so fucking perfect wrapped around my dick."

Then his hands are in my hair, cupping the back of my head, encouraging me to swallow more of his length, so I relax my throat and allow him to guide his cock deeper into my mouth.

Jackson

"Jesus, Smokey," I can't help but gasp. "Your mouth feels so fucking perfect wrapped around my dick."

I barely get the words out before I'm gripping her head between my palms, urging her perfect little mouth to swallow me down until I hit the back of her throat. I don't have the biggest dick in the world by any means, but I've got a girthy six and a half inches that hasn't ever let me down. Today is no exception.

She hums in appreciation, rubbing her tongue along the shaft, and my knees go weak as my vision blurs from the pleasure. Which is a damn shame because the sight of her on her knees before me, eating up my dick while I stare down into her expressive, blue eyes is something I want seared onto the insides of my eyelids forever. So that I can replay this moment, over and over, every time I blink, for the rest of my life.

She eases her head back slowly, gradually revealing the inches of my cock, shiny with her saliva. Kissing the swollen tip before lapping up my pre-cum once again, her eyes never leave my face as she grips the back of my thighs and pulls herself forward, sinking me back into the depths of her mouth until her lips meet my pelvis.

The girl can suck cock like a fucking pro, a thought that causes gratitude to war with self-hatred within me when I recall everything she's been through.

"Fuck!" I choke out, all thoughts of self-loathing evaporating when she uses one hand to gently cup and massage my balls, while the other jacks my shaft up and down, adding delicious friction to the warm, wet suction she's already applying. "You want my cum to run down that pretty little throat?" I grunt out, but of course, she doesn't answer. Instead, she hollows her cheeks, sucking harder, sharpening the knife of pleasure that stabs through me.

I can feel myself losing my battle with control as I wind her braid around my fist. Holding her head still, I piston my hips in and out of her mouth, my dick sliding between her wet, slobbery lips at an unsteady pace. "Huh, Little Smoke Show?" I taunt as I continue fucking her delectable mouth. "You want me to quench your thirst and let you taste how good you make me feel?" She hums again in response, nice and long, and the vibration is my undoing. But instead of giving her what she wants, I pull out at the last second, baptizing her with my seed.

Hot ropes of cum lace her chin and neck, dripping onto her cleavage as she sputters and gasps for breath. "I had to see what you looked like covered in me, the way I'm covered in you," I pant, answering the question I can already see forming in her eyes. "And now you definitely need the shower first." I add with a smile, holding out a hand to help her up.

"What if we both shower first?" The tentative question takes me by surprise, and she looks away shyly as she rubs my essence into her skin. It takes a moment to form a response as I watch, trying to process what she's offering.

"You mean together." I state it like a fact, but she nods her head anyway, chewing nervously on her bottom lip.

Reaching up with my thumb, I tug the pillowy bit of flesh free of her teeth. Then, coating the very same thumb with some of the lingering wetness on her cheek, I paint her bottom lip with it, watching in fascination as her little pink tongue immediately pokes out to lick it away. "If that's what you want." I finally tell her, my voice coming out a raspy whisper.

Without another word, she turns and walks to the bathroom leaving me helpless to do anything but follow.

Smokey

Jackson shadows me into the bathroom, and the limited space feels even smaller once I'm sharing it with him. With my back still turned, I eyeball the bathtub and shower combo. A glossy, blue curtain hanging from a silver rod is the only promise of privacy anywhere in the room. Directly across from the shower is a long, wide mirror with double sinks carved into the faux marble counter beneath. In front of me, between the other main fixtures, sits the toilet with a row of shelving filled with towels and extra toilet paper suspended above. Other than the hair dryer mounted on the wall, and the tiny, complimentary soaps on the counter by the sink, there's nothing else in here with us. Not even oxygen.

In the mirror, I watch breathlessly as his reflection reaches for the end of my braid, removing the hair tie, and carefully unwinding the tresses. His touch is gentle as his fingers comb through the strands, and I have to suppress a moan every time his fingertips graze my scalp.

"May I undress you?" He's so close, I can feel his body heat at my back since I haven't convinced myself to turn around yet. Where did he even find the air to speak?

"Smokey." Gently taking me by the shoulders, he turns me to face him. Staring at the wall of his chest now, one of his big warm hands reaches up to tilt my chin until we're making eye contact. "'No,' is a full sentence." He looks at me seriously. "You can say it now if you want to, and I'll go. I won't be mad."

No is a full sentence... Time seems to slow as the words replay in my mind like a ripple across still water. *I won't be mad.*

I'm struck suddenly with the knowledge that if I did, in fact, say, "*No, stop, I don't want to do this anymore,*" he'd turn around and walk right out of the bathroom and leave me alone. This whole encounter would be over, I just have to say the word.

What a heady and powerful realization.

Emboldened by this brand new awareness, I finally find my voice.

"I've cried the word 'no' so many times, and it never made a difference." He swallows thickly, and I'm momentarily distracted by the way the muscles in his throat flex with the action. "Now, I think I'd like to know what it feels like to say yes."

He cups my face tenderly, caressing my cheekbones with his thumbs.

"As you wish," he whispers, but the significance is lost on me as he takes my lips in another breath-stealing, heart-pounding, world-bending kiss.

We break apart, gasping for breath in tandem, as he bunches the fabric of my dress in his hands, and I raise my arms to facilitate him pulling the garment off over my head. I stand before him completely bare, adorned only by my scars and the brazen red streaks of my womanhood on my thighs. I squeeze them together in an attempt to staunch the flow, and fight the deep-seated urge to cover myself with my hands. No matter how much I want this, it's still so hard to fight the shame that's been ingrained in me.

His scorching gaze travels over my body, igniting fires along my skin, leaving no part of me unburned by the heat in his eyes. Suddenly, without warning, he presses a palm into the roundest part of my belly. Where so many of the scars reside. Caressing my ruined flesh, he asks, "How did you get them?"

"Uncle Mike." I whisper his name quickly as if saying it too slow or too loud will somehow conjure him.

"Tell me," he demands, and I'm surprised by how much I want to.

"When I bleed, I know that I'm..." I stop to swallow, bracing myself for what I'm about to share with him. "I'm unclean. That's what he always used to say. It's a manifestation of all my sins... My punishment for being a woman."

His eyes are fierce as he looks down at me.

"You know that's not true, don't you?"

All I can do is stare blankly at him.

"Go on," he urges, his voice gruff with emotion.

"I was fourteen the first time it happened."

The words come easier than I expected, like I'm meant to spill all of my shame at his feet. It feels surprisingly cathartic to finally let it all go and say it out loud. "I didn't even really know what was happening to me..." My words stall out, because how embarrassing is it to admit that I wasn't even aware of my own bodily functions. "He tried washing me out with a bar of soap." Jackson's fingers flex suddenly on my abdomen, but he doesn't remove his hand, and I'm grateful for that.

"When that obviously didn't work, he became enraged. He beat me until I couldn't walk, all the while screaming that I was the Devil's whore." Taking another fortifying breath, I avoid his deeply searching gaze. "After that, I tried desperately to hide it from him whenever I started...but my body wasn't my own. It belonged to him. One time he brought an old Swiss army knife to my bed..."

This time I stop because what comes next is so awful, I have to steel myself to say the words.

"It's okay, Smokey. It's just a memory. He can't hurt you anymore."

His steady voice grounds me, and I take another much-needed breath.

What is it about this man that allows him to steal my breath one minute, yet give it back to me the next?

"He had tied me up before waking me with the blade, raping me with it first, saying that if I wanted to bleed, he'd make sure it never stopped." Jackson's fingertips dig into my hips suddenly, pulling me close and pressing in hard enough to leave bruises, but I don't tell him to stop or let go. It feels good to be connected to him at this moment, baring the darkest parts of myself and having him hold me closer in spite of them. It gives me the courage to finish my brutal tale.

"When he grew tired of that, he started cutting into me, swearing that he would remove the evil from my womb one way or another. I probably would have died that night if Kelly hadn't stopped him, the only real kindness she ever showed me.

"At the nearest urgent care, which was still far enough away I passed out and almost bled to death in the back of the truck, my step-mother told all the attending that I had done it to myself..." My voice wavers with emotion as I confess my ultimate sin, "...and when I woke up several hours after being rushed into emergency surgery, I was too weak and afraid to speak up and tell anyone the truth. " I can't stop the tears from spilling over now. "I won't ever be able to have children, and those people will never believe that it's not my fault."

"Shh, Smokey, it's alright—"

"Alright?!" I can't believe he just said that. He doesn't *know*. He doesn't understand. "Weren't you listening?" I ask hysterically. "I can't have babies. Who could possibly want me now?" I squeeze my eyes shut, blocking him and everything else out, but they flutter back open when I feel his warm, rough palms gently framing my face.

"I do, Smokey." Jackson's liquid brown eyes bounce back and forth between mine with a burning intensity. "And I'll never let anyone hurt you again."

He seals his declaration with a searing, healing kiss, and in the midst of it, I can feel myself tumbling over some sort of irrevocable cliff. I don't entirely understand it, but I know there's no going back now.

Jackson

Her words cut into me like the knife that was used to mar her perfect flesh, and I know I'll bear the marks on my soul the same way she carries them on her body. Despite the horrors she's suffered, she tastes like hope and desperation, and I meet the flavors of her longing with my own.

The kiss ends too soon when her lips leave mine, and she breathlessly says, "I showed you mine, now show me yours." She gestures to my clothes with a shy smile, raising a challenging eyebrow with a smirk that I'm eager to kiss off her face, but she's right. I'm desperate to feel her naked skin against mine.

Without wasting any more time, I kick off my pants, still undone from before, while simultaneously pulling my shirt over my head with one hand. It takes me less than five seconds to strip down and pull her naked body flush against mine.

She yelps in surprise when our bodies collide, but I swallow the sound with another hungry kiss. Now that I've had a taste of her, it doesn't seem like I'll ever be able to get enough.

When I finally release her, I whip her petite little body around, bringing her back to my front while we face the large mirror over the counter. Lifting her off the ground a little with my arm around her waist, I notch my erection in the space between her thighs, and press her up against the edge of the counter, leaning into her with my body weight to hold her in place. She's so much smaller than me, it's easy to move her around just where I want her. Like a perfect little doll.

"Fuck, Smokey. You feel so good against me," I grit out as I roll my hips into her ass, rubbing my cock against her slick opening.

"Jackson..." My name is a whine, a plea, and a prayer.

"Look at us," I tell her as my other hand forms a necklace around her slender neck, holding her to me. She obeys me immediately, opening her eyes lazily to drag them up our bodies to meet mine in the mirror. "Look at how beautiful you are pinned against me, waiting for your pleasure." I whisper the words in her ear while I watch her watching us.

Taking a small step back, I allow her feet to touch the floor again as I press gently between her shoulder blades, pushing until she's bending forward over the countertop, slightly arching her back as she rests on her forearms.

"Don't move, and don't take your eyes off of mine in the mirror. I want you to see how magnificent I think you feel wrapped around my dick." Her cheeks fill with that innocent blush color I love, and I can't help the way it pulls the corners of my mouth into a wicked grin. "Now, lift up onto those toes, babygirl," I demand, and my cock grows impossibly harder when she immediately obeys. "You're such a good girl for me, Smokey. Are you ready to be rewarded?" I palm her perfectly round ass, unable to keep from squeezing and kneading the plump flesh.

"Yes, please!" she whimpers, and I nudge her legs wider apart to accommodate my size.

"Watch me, Little Smoke Show, while I make you feel good," I remind her before squatting a little to line my aching cock up with her dripping entrance.

I don't take my eyes off her reflection for a second as I push into her from behind. Inch by slow, agonizing inch. I watch, completely enraptured, as she stares back at me, her mouth going wide in a silent scream as I stretch her tight cunt around my solid cock, not stopping until I'm fully seated to the hilt, lifting her feet off the ground again.

The split in her bottom lip has reopened, and a crimson bead forms there, taunting me from my position behind her. I wish I could lick the pretty little jewel away before sucking that luscious lip into my mouth and biting it again myself.

"Let me hear you, pretty girl. Show me how much you like being impaled on this fat cock."

"Jackson, please!" she whimpers. "I'm so full." Her dilated eyes struggle to focus on mine in the mirror, hardly any blue showing around her large, dark pupils.

"Please, what?" I ask playfully, bending over her to nuzzle the spot behind her ear and press kisses to the sensitive skin there, enjoying the sensation of her pussy pulsing erratically around my cock.

"Pleeeaaasssse..." she begs again, drawing the word out as her hips begin to move involuntarily, seeking the friction she so desperately needs.

"Please, what?" I ask again, whispering deviously into her ear. "Use your words, Pretty Girl."

"Fuck me, Jackson!" The words tumble uninhibited from her lips. "Fuck me, and make me forget about everything else but you."

She doesn't need to ask twice.

Snaking a hand between the front of her body and the counter top, I rub my fingers through her slick folds until I find the little hidden bundle of nerves that has her pussy clenching around me like a vise.

"Fuck, you're so tight." I press more wet kisses to her neck while I begin to fuck her the way we both need. "You feel so fucking good wrapped around my dick. You know that, Smokey?"

"Jackson, I..." She stops talking as her mouth drops open on a loud, unintelligible moan, and her eyes flutter closed.

"You what, baby? Open up those pretty blue eyes, and tell me what you need."

"I don't... .I can't... I don't... I need..." She pants, seeming to lose her train of thought with every deep thrust, encouraging me to pick up the pace.

"Oh God. Oh God. Oh God," she chants with each stroke.

"That's right, baby. Tell Him who this pussy belongs to."

I thrust savagely into her. Hard, punishing strokes that have her body bouncing on the glassy surface.

"Jackson!" Her legs shake as she screams my name, her vaginal walls convulsing around me until the cream of her release drips out around my cock. That sight, coupled with the indecent sound of my cum soaked dick sliding in and out of her wet channel, is my undoing. My hips move erratically, pounding at a wild pace until I follow her over the edge with a primal roar.

Smokey

Jackson's large form is draped over the back of mine, pinning my hair between our sweaty bodies. I'm pressed into the unforgiving counter top with each deep breath he takes, but I hardly even register these uncomfortable sensations as I bask in the euphoria of the moment.

I didn't know sex could be like that; *feel* like that. When he reached between my legs and rubbed that spot— I swear it felt like I was being electrocuted. But like, in a good way. Like his dick was a magic candle lighting a fuse inside me. I thought I was going to explode. I think maybe I did.

My cheeks warm, but for the first time...I don't feel ashamed.

Jackson places a gentle kiss on my right shoulder before stepping back a little, giving me space to plant my feet firmly on the floor. An obscene squelching sound fills the room as his spent cock slips from my body, and pink tinted goo drips immediately out of me to splatter on the white tile floor below. I don't have to see my reflection to know that my whole face is turning red.

"Hey." He turns me around, tipping my chin up so that I meet his eyes.

"You are not wicked, dirty, or unclean." My vision begins to blur with tears, but I don't look away. How can I, when I'm finally being *seen*?

"You are just a woman. And you are capable of doing everything a man can't. Do you understand me? You have *nothing* to be ashamed of." He speaks with such conviction. "Do you believe that?"

I nod my head because I don't trust myself to speak without dissolving into an even bigger mess of tears.

"Good," he says, using his thumbs to wipe the wetness from my cheeks. "Now, let's get you cleaned up."

AFTER INSISTING HE wash my hair, and every other part of me, Jackson now sits behind me on the bed, caging me between his tree-trunk thighs as he gently combs through my tresses. Rather than being a deterrent, his size is a comfort to me. I feel protected, yet oddly powerful as he sits, a wall of raw masculinity at my back, daintily brushing my hair.

"Are you sure you want me to pick what we watch? I don't even know what's good." I ask as I lazily flip through TV channels, completely overwhelmed by the sheer volume of choices. "Are this many channels even necessary? I mean, doesn't anyone read anymore?"

"Why would anyone pick up a book when they can just watch the movie?"

I can't tell if he's being serious or not from behind me, but I give him the only answer I have either way.

"Books may be the only way some people have to escape."

My statement falls like a stone, unintentionally crushing the fragile, light-hearted mood between us. There's a beat of weighted silence before he quietly responds.

"You're right. Books were my escape in prison."

Warmth spreads through me at this unexpected understanding we share.

Desperate to recapture the lighter tone from before, I grasp at the threads of our conversation. "Someone should really make a list of all of these channels," I joke. "I've already forgotten half of what I've seen."

"Actually..." He smirks as he takes the remote from me, hitting a little, blue button that reads, "Guide."

Suddenly, the screen is filled with columns of blue boxes, different titles and time stamps labeling each one.

"Oh!" I gasp in wonder and surprise.

"Just use the up and down arrows," he uses his thumb to gesture over the keypad of the remote, "to scroll up or down." He clicks the 'up' arrow a few times, showing me how it works before offering the device back to me. I take it back from him, probably more amazed than I should be.

He turns his attention back to my wet hair that he's now combed, and moves on to trying to braid it. Badly, I might add. It takes practice working with unruly, curly hair, even when it's wet. It's cute to watch him try, though.

Unable to make a decision on my own, I begin listing movie titles out loud, telling him to stop me when he hears something he likes:

"Wedding Crashers, The Other Guys, Sweet Home Alabama, Horrible Bosses, The Expendables, Armageddon, The Notebook . . ."

"Wait, what was the last one?" he asks with a glint in his eye.

"The Notebook?"

"No, before that." I look back at the screen.

"Armageddon?"

"Yes! That. We're watching that." He smirks again and seems excited for some reason.

Selecting it, I ask, "What's it about?" My curiosity piqued by his behavior. "The end of the world," he supplies with a smile as the actors fill the screen.

A young man in his underwear is being chased by an older one with a shotgun through a maze of steaming pipes, grates, and other heavy-looking machinery. A young woman's face appears, shouting, *"Harry! This is not funny!"*

I gasp in shock, shooting my gaze over to Jackson, who's smiling at me like the Big Bad Wolf who ate Little Red's granny.

"She looks like me!" I blurt with enthusiasm. "Or...I guess I look like her."

"Exactly, Liv," he says with a wink before we both return our attention to the screen.

The movie captivates me. I'm enthralled by the actress who shares my face, and invested in the relationship between the single father just trying to raise and protect his only daughter. The heartbreaking depth of their love depicts a bond I could have had but will never experience. At least not in this lifetime.

When the credits roll, I wait, eyes glued to the screen, anxious to learn the actress's name that I look so much like. Aerosmith's "I Don't Want To Miss A Thing," fills the room as I read the name *Liv Tyler* and find myself swept up in the emotions the song evokes.

Glancing over at Jackson, I find his eyes already closed, his eyelashes fanned perfectly against his cheeks, his chest rising and falling with the deep, easy rhythm of sleep. With an ironic sigh, I switch the television off, blanketing the room in only relative silence and darkness.

Light from the hallway streams in from the crack under the door, and I can hear what sounds like a child shouting before it's punctuated by the loud thumps of running footsteps. Scooting down under the covers next to Jackson, I tuck myself into his body so that he's the big spoon at my back. The messy braid he did for me earlier presses into the side of my head as the lyrics from the song play on repeat in my mind:

"I don't want to close my eyes,
I don't want to fall asleep
Cause I'd miss you, babe.
And I don't wanna miss a thing."

I really don't want to close my eyes or fall asleep. Because then I could miss one of the moments I have left with Jackson...and I don't want to miss a single breath.

Jackson

I wake up early, feeling rested in a way I don't think I've ever experienced before. The hollowness I've carried around in my chest for so long is absent. For the first time in my life, I feel...content. It's as if everything is finally as it should be, and I'm finally whole. I shake my head in bewilderment because that sounds crazy. Even still, I can't shake the feeling. It just seems as if everything is going to be okay from now on. I cut my eyes to the right and find what I suspect is the reason why.

She's sleeping so soundly beside me, a little snore whistles out of her nose with every exhale. It's the most adorable fucking sound I've ever heard, and that's how I know I've completely lost my head over her. Maybe even my heart.

We covered a lot of ground last night. She finally opened up to me, sharing some truly horrific things. But just because we've slept together doesn't mean she wants to stay with me. She might need some convincing.

Sitting up slowly, I run my fingers through my hair as I carefully ease my weight off the mattress. I don't want to disturb the little sleeping beauty. If I'm quick about it, I can have breakfast ready and waiting here for her before she even wakes up.

As I dress quietly in my customary jeans, boots, and plain, black t-shirt, my eyes catch the little pile of dirty clothes Smokey assembled last night after our time together in the shower. Seeing our belongings combined in such a domestic way feels profoundly intimate, and I'm struck by how much I enjoy seeing her things blended with mine.

I spy my gray towel in the mix, and wonder when she snuck it out of my bag. The one she accidentally got blood on back at the truck stop shower. Was that only yesterday? My perception of time feels skewed because even though it's only been three days, my soul seems to recognize hers. It's as if I've always been waiting to find her, and now that I have... Fuck, it's like I can finally breathe again, inhaling for the first time since I found out about Amy.

After tossing the dirty clothes into my laundry bag, I start to leave as silently as possible before remembering how terrified she looked at the idea of being alone last night. What if she wakes up and finds me gone, with some of our things missing? The last thing I want to do is give her a reason to panic.

Scanning the room for solutions, my gaze lands on the desk where there's a pen sitting next to a little notepad with the green Holiday Inn logo centered at the top of the page. Only after scribbling a quick message and leaving it on my pillow for her to find, do I exit the room, holding onto the door so that it shuts slowly and quietly behind me. Stopping at the front desk, I drop off the laundry before heading out on my mission to find food.

When I return a little later carrying a bag from a local cafe in one hand, and a carrier of coffees in the other, the bed is empty, but I can hear water running from behind the closed bathroom door. Flipping the TV on to fill the silence, I start pulling food out of the bag to situate on the little dining table while I wait for her to emerge.

I know she likes pancakes because she ordered them from that first greasy spoon we stopped at in the middle of nowhere on the first day. I also know she likes peanut butter, so I made sure to get some on the side, in case she wants it to go with her syrup. As I go about setting up our breakfast, a familiar face on the ten o'clock morning news unexpectedly snags my attention.

"Authorities have been looking for Smokey Waters since Wednesday afternoon, where she was reportedly taken from an old, local truck stop off of Highway 278 in Georgia." An image of Smokey's face fills the screen.

It's an older, grainy picture, but still. I'd recognize those haunted angel eyes anywhere. She looks younger, thinner, gazing at the camera with a dazed and empty expression that makes bile rise in the back of my throat. The world begins to bend around me, and a pit opens up in my stomach as the reporter continues her story.

"The seventeen-year-old was last seen wearing a turquoise blue tank top, black denim shorts, and hot pink sandals..." Smokey quietly exits the bathroom as the woman on the television goes on, but all I can hear is static in my ears while one thought circles around in my brain. *Seventeen...she's only seventeen.*

"Jackson, I can explain." Her soft voice cuts through the panic taking over my mind and I pin her with a glare.

"Explain what? You lied. It's pretty self-explanatory." My voice sounds sharp and cold, too loud in the small space, but I can't help it. She played me. I've been over here possessed like a mad man trying to earn her trust when she was keeping secrets the whole time.

She was too young for you even when you thought she was twenty. But at least then I thought she was legal. I argue uselessly with myself. Amy flashes through my mind, sneering at me, reminding me that I'm no better than my father after all, and I close my eyes as my stomach turns with revulsion so strong it nearly doubles me over where I stand. *She's just a fucking kid.*

"Was any of it real?" I ask, turning on her. She looks taken aback, as if I just slapped her.

"O-of course it was. It is," she sputters. "You think I could do this to myself?" She asks, lifting a shaking hand to her stomach to cover the scars I know are there. "You think *this,*" she grips the soft flesh of her belly to emphasize the word, "is *fake?*" Her voice sounds incredulous as it trembles, rising in volume as her cheeks fill with color. "*You* took *me*, remember? I didn't ask for *any* of this!"

"You asked me for last night." I force the words out, and they fall heavy between us, a tangible weight that makes every breath feel like I'm trying to pull mud into my lungs.

"Jackson, I–"

"Just save it, okay?" My voice still sounds too loud, but I can't seem to control my volume. I have to get out of here, away from her, before I suffocate under the weight of my self-loathing.

In an angry chaotic rush, I begin gathering my things. "I've wasted so much time trying to make you feel safe, trying to make you believe that you can trust me." I laugh bitterly at myself. "I never even considered that I shouldn't trust *you.*"

"Just wait! Give me a minute to explain–"

"I have!" It's a roar as I fling my arms wide in exasperation. When she stumbles back a step in fear, I feel a pang of regret, but I bury it beneath the avalanche of shame and self-disgust rising within me. "All I asked for was the truth, and in return, that's what I gave to you. I just didn't expect to be the one in danger of being manipulated, you know? I actually bought into your doe-eyed Bambi routine. I never thought a *child*," I spit the word at her, "could be so cunning. So ruthless.

But I guess I should have known just by looking in a mirror, sometimes monsters just make other monsters, don't they, Liv?"

Smokey

S *ometimes monsters just make other monsters, don't they, Liv?* The question nearly levels me where I stand, but the wall behind me offers much-needed support as his hateful words break over me.

"I just wanted...to know what... it felt like...to choose." I choke out, desperate to make him understand.

"You just don't get it, do you?" His voice rises, sneering at me through my anguish. "You're just a God damn kid! You fear a man's touch, even as you crave it, because neglect, sex, and violence are all you've ever known."

"Until now." I try to respond, but it only comes out as a trembling whisper. I'm not afraid of him. Not anymore. Not after *everything*.

I'm only afraid of the things he's saying now.

Uncaring of the damage he inflicts upon me, he sucks in a deep breath, letting it go in a *whoosh*, causing his shoulders to sag in defeat.

"You only want to stay with me because no one has ever protected you and made you feel safe before. *That's* what you're afraid of losing. Not me, Liv." His voice cracks on the stupid, little nickname, just like the foolish organ in my chest.

"No! You're wrong!" I yell through my sobs, sliding down the wall and covering my ears like a toddler throwing a temper tantrum. I don't want to hear the truth anymore. It hurts more than I anticipated. But he only ignores my childish behavior and goes on.

"And me? I've just been chasing after Amy's ghost through you. Like saving you would somehow absolve me of the sins of my past." He chuckles again, but it's full of self-loathing. "And all I have to show for it is a new stain on my soul." He shakes his head sardonically as he walks to the door. I crawl after him like a lost puppy, begging him not to go.

"Please? Please don't do this, please don't go. I don't know how to do anything on my own. I have nothing!" Panic has my voice rising hysterically.

He turns back to me, but he doesn't let go of the handle. He studies me for so long I start to think that I did it. I actually convinced him to change his mind and stay with me.

"You have your freedom," he declares before walking out of my life.

The quiet snick of the door closing seems to echo through the room, detonating like a bomb against my already frayed nerves. My entire life, everything I know, has gone up in smoke, and I'm completely and totally alone.

Part of my brain screams at me to *move*! To run after him and keep begging him to stay. But I can't seem to propel myself forward. Instead, I crumple in a heap on the floor, clutching my stomach as I fold into the fetal position. Squeezing my eyes shut, I shake my head from side to side, like my mind is an Etch-A-Sketch and I can erase everything that just happened.

Even Uncle Mike's torture was easier to bear than this. At least I knew it would eventually end.

Two Years Later

Smokey

I lie on my back, staring up at the ceiling all but counting the seconds to sunrise. Puffing out my cheeks, I blow out a deep breath. This is it. My twentieth birthday. I'm officially the age I lied about being two years ago, when a handsome stranger snatched me off the side of a road and changed my life forever.

I'm underwhelmed.

I thought I would feel different somehow. Like maybe I'd have some of that infamous closure my therapist is always talking about.

Sometimes, I still wonder what would have happened if I hadn't lied to him. Would he have treated me differently? Would I have wanted him to? Would he have stayed? I crinkle my nose in disgust.

I know better than to believe in fairy tales.

Suddenly, a rooster begins to crow at me from my nightstand, the obnoxious sound choice I selected as my early morning alarm dispelling thoughts and feelings that are best left in the past. Swiping my phone screen silences the sound, and I groan as I peel myself from the mattress.

Once standing, I stretch my hands high over my head to elongate my spine, opening my mouth to let out a huge yawn at the same time. My oversized T-shirt rides up my thighs with the motion and declares, *"I'll sleep when I'm dead,"* which is apt because of my insomnia.

It often feels like I won't get any rest until I finally keel over and die. Not that I think about dying. Not anymore, at least. It hasn't been easy, but I'm healing and building a life for myself out of the wreckage that Jackson left behind a little over two years ago.

After he left me at that Holiday Inn in Mississippi, I couldn't see the light anymore. I wanted to die more than ever before. I might have actually succeeded in ending it all that day if the maid hadn't discovered me first.

An angel in disguise with warm, brown skin, deep laugh lines, and a maternal streak a country mile wide, Grace Hurley found me unconscious in the hotel room shower, rivers of crimson bleeding from vertical cuts on the insides of my forearms.

A force to be reckoned with, she wasted no time making tourniquets out of towels and dialing 911. She even bullied her way into the ambulance with me, never letting go of my hand, despite the very real repercussions to her job.

She stayed by my side at the hospital, asking intelligently pointed questions that gave the impression of a seasoned medical professional. She watched over me, defending me when I couldn't defend myself, and when I asked her why she would do all that for a perfect stranger, she simply replied, "Because it's what Jesus would do."

Her unerring compassion and unwavering loyalty throughout the mandatory psyche hold had me spilling my guts to her in no time, one sordid detail after the other.

Opening up was cathartic. Once I started, it was like a verbal flood I couldn't stop.

I told her about staring wistfully at Jackson's truck, longing for an escape, when the man in question stopped next to me and lit a cigarette. I told her how big he was, and how it didn't scare me like it should have. Not until I heard the roar of his engine coming for me.

I admitted to her that even while I ran out of fear, I couldn't stop the fire of excitement that bloomed within me. It was like he had read my mind while we stood side by side on that hot sidewalk.

Remarkably, the older woman didn't judge me. She heard all of my shameful confessions with an easy acceptance, offering forgiveness for each sinful indiscretion until I had purged myself of everything.

In the days that followed, I found myself emotionally relying on Grace more and more, soaking up her maternal affection like a plant does sunlight. Terrified of being alone, I was tempted to stay with her, but in the end I couldn't bring myself to keep taking advantage of her kindness any longer than necessary. It took a little while to pull myself together without her unending support, but thanks to the little bit of cash she gave me, I managed to get my hands on a bus ticket and finally make it to New Orleans.

Stepping off of a dirty Greyhound, I took my first breath of the thick, sultry air. I had almost convinced myself that I'd be able to sense my mother's presence or something, but of course that didn't happen.

Grow up, Liv, I remember thinking, hating myself for the way the name stuck in my subconscious. Try as I might, I couldn't get his voice out of my head. Maybe I wasn't trying very hard. Maybe I'm still not.

The scant bit of money I had didn't go very far, so it wasn't long before I was seeking refuge at a homeless shelter. The first few days weren't so bad. I had food to eat and a cot to sleep on. I kept to myself mostly, but I was really trying to utilize the resources the shelter provided to get back on my feet.

Then, one night I woke up with a heavy body on top of mine and putrid breath in my face as my attacker muttered something about teaching the cock tease a lesson. I remember praying to God, begging him to save me just one more time... Then the weight was lifted, and I didn't think, I just bolted, never looking back. I wasn't interested in trading one house of horrors for another.

Been there, done that.

With no money and wary of the shelters, I took my chances on the streets, sticking to the shadows and avoiding crowds as often as possible. It wasn't until Annette, a fellow insomniac, was out on her balcony enjoying a pre-dawn cigarette that I was caught sifting through her garbage. The row of trash cans outside of her bakery were some of my favorites, always smelling of chocolate, coffee, and fresh baked bread.

I can still remember the way the cherry glowed, softly illuminating her delicate features as she called out to me in a foreign language. Startled, I froze in place as my eyes searched for the source of the melodic voice. Mesmerized by her presence, I was transported to that first encounter with Jackson standing just outside of Trusty Rusty'z. Caught somewhere between the past and the present, I was responding to the mysterious, ethereal woman before I could stop myself.

Stamping out her cigarette as I tried to apologize, she waved off my words and told me to wait there before she slipped inside a window and disappeared. I still don't know what held me there, or why I listened, but when she reappeared on the ground floor gesturing for me to come inside, I didn't hesitate.

A survivor herself, Annette saw something familiar in me that night. To this day, I still don't quite understand what compelled her to take me in, but I know it has something to do with the gnarly scar on her collar bone that she refuses to talk about. She told me about it once, but it was all in Creole, so I didn't understand a word of it. I'm better with the unique dialect now, but she just brushes me off whenever I ask about it, despite knowing everything about me.

In the grand scheme of things, I guess it doesn't really matter. I'm just grateful to have a friend, a home, and a job that I enjoy and actually seem to be pretty good at.

Annette is the owner of *La Petite Mort*, a tiny, little cafe and bakery with a prime location in the middle of The French Quarter. Despite its minuscule size, the business usually has a line going out the door for most of the day. Translated to English, the name means *The Little Death*, which she informed me is what the French affectionately call an orgasm.

"That is why the slogan is, '*Good enough to die for*,' non?" She had told me, her soft, accented voice full of amusement at the time.

I've been eagerly learning from her ever since, soaking up her *je ne sais quoi* as often as possible. She's like the mother I never had, but when I told her that, she laughed, saying that she was no one's mother, but she could definitely be my dishy big sister. She's been like family to me ever since.

Dragging myself downstairs to the cafe from the cozy, two-bedroom apartment we share above, I hit the lights and try not to have a heart attack when Wheezy, the asthmatic calico I talked Annette into letting me adopt last month, darts past me. I gasp, slapping a hand to my chest over my pounding heartbeat as the grumpy blur ascends into the shadows above.

"Well, good morning to you too," I grumble as I begin prepping the life-saving liquid the world needs to be able to function properly throughout the day.

As the strong aroma permeates the small space, I take a moment to close my eyes and inhale. God, I love that smell. I love the coffee here. It's different in The Paris of The South. We add chicory root to the coffee beans to give it a richer, earthier, nuttier flavor.

I read a popular romance last year that had a funny quote about thanking the bean gods for coffee. Inhaling again, I can relate to the sentiment, but I'll stay thanking the root gods for their many uses. I mean, who can resist the versatility of the potato? I rest my case.

"Happy birthday, *cher*." Annette's melodious creole cadence floats to me as she descends the stairs into the small restaurant wearing nothing but her blush-colored silk robe.

"Thanks." I send her a smile over my shoulder as I fix myself a cup of coffee, adding a splash of cream to the fragrant, steaming liquid. "I didn't wake you, did I?"

"*Oui,* of course you did!" she laughs as she answers. "These walls are paper thin." She flaps a hand around, gesturing to the space around us.

"Don't I know it." I smirk at her as she yawns sleepily, relieving me of the warm mug I carry and inhaling deeply before taking a sip. She hums in appreciation before walking away with my cup, causing me to roll my eyes at her back before turning to make another. "What time did Marco leave last night?" I ask as she makes herself comfortable at our favorite table.

"Oh, that wasn't Marco," she informs me, "It was Jonathon...and Joanne." She waggles her eyebrows suggestively.

"Jonathon and Joanne? Like a married couple?" I counter in disbelief. She laughs, saying something about my innocence in her native tongue before clarifying, "Brother and sister, *teet fee*. Twins, in fact."

"What?" I gasp in total shock. "That's like incest. Wait, no! It's *twincest*." I cackle at my own joke.

"*Ça suffit*!" she playfully scolds me. "You shouldn't yuck someone else's yum, *ma belle*. There are many different things out there waiting to be experienced and enjoyed. One only needs to be willing."

I look at her skeptically, trying and failing not to recall the way it felt when Jackson pulled a tampon from my body with his teeth. Yeah, I'm definitely not unwilling to try things.

Almost as if reading my mind she asks, "Now, what shall we try for today, hmm?"

"Well..." I draw the word out as I bring my mind back to pastry prep. "I've already mastered croissants, eclairs, madeleines, and macaroons, so I was thinking we could finally try the *Mille-feuille*?" I ask hopefully.

"*If you think you are ready*." She replies in Creole, but after nearly two years with her, I'm pretty proud of how much of the culture I've been able to obtain.

"Yeah, well, I'm hoping if I start learning now, I can be a pro when Mardi Gras comes around again."

"It can be very difficult to get all the layers just right."

"I know, that's why I'm coming to the best baker in the whole wide world." I bat my eyelashes playfully with the praise, causing her musical laugh to trill out again.

"*Oui*, alright. But only because you have the gift, which makes you such a pleasure to teach."

"And everyone knows that Annette does nothing if it doesn't bring her pleasure," I tease.

"*Mais, oui!*" She laughs again, and I can't help but join in, basking in the glow of our friendship as we get to work on the delicate pastry dough.

Jackson

I thought leaving Amy behind in my attempt to escape my piece of shit father would be my biggest regret in this life, but it turns out, I was wrong. Repeating my mistake, and deserting Smokey that day more than two years ago has got to be the worst thing I've ever done.

After getting some distance and clearing my head, it was easy to see the way I overreacted. I didn't even give her a chance to explain. I was just so scared and disgusted, I went straight into fight mode. I turned on her, and even felt vindicated when she begged me to stay, and I left her behind. Like I was teaching her some kind of lesson for lying to me. But the reality that sickened me is the same one that explained her actions. She was just a kid. Just like Amy had been...And she owed me nothing. Not even the truth.

After spending the night in my truck, I tried to go back the next morning, sick with guilt over the things I had said and the way I left things, but no one seemed to have any memory of me, or my Liv Tyler look-alike. Not even the night shift clerk who checked me in with her blood still staining my face.

It was clear I was missing something, but no one was going to tell me what.

Out of ideas, I even tried pounding on the door of the room we had shared until the guests in the room next door called the front desk to complain. Between being given the option of leaving on my own or waiting for a police escort, I went out to my truck where I spent the next few days watching the entrance, hoping and praying for a glimpse of her short, curvy silhouette, but again, she was like Amy to me— Nothing but a ghost.

In her absence, I felt lost. Crawling into bottle after bottle, attempting to hide from the beautiful specters that haunted my every waking thought. I drank until their faces began to blend together in my mind, warping them both into one great loss. I drank until I forgot my own name and why I was grieving in the first place. Then, one day, I reached for a bottle that came up empty.

They all were. Just like me.

In my rare and accidental moment of sobriety, I was forced to face myself, and I didn't really like what I saw; the patterns I had created for whenever I felt like my control was threatened. Feeling sick, uncertain, and insecure, I convinced myself that Gibbs would know what to do. He had saved me once before, he could do it again. I wasn't exactly thrilled at the prospect of returning to prison, but he wasn't about to get out, so that meant I had to go to him.

The officers at intake had no problem making things uncomfortable for me, cracking jokes about how I must have missed servicing the other inmates and couldn't stay away. I let their unoriginal attempts at getting under my skin roll off of me like water on a duck, even when they got a little too familiar during the pat down. I knew they were only hoping to get a rise out of me, and I wasn't about to give them the satisfaction. I had more important things on my mind than what a bunch of bored men in uniforms thought of me.

When I was finally escorted to the visitation area, Gibbs was already there waiting for me.

"YOU LOOK LIKE SHIT, kid."

"Yeah, thanks." I run my hands half haphazardly through my greasy hair while lowering myself into the plastic chair across from the grizzled old man. Then we just sit there in silence, him staring at me while I stare blankly at the table.

"Well," he sighs, rapping the table top with his knuckles. "What the hell do you want, son? I ain't got all day."

I can't help the smile that tries to tug at the corner of my mouth. It feels foreign on my face.

"What are you talking about, old timer? Last time I did the math, you still had eighteen years left of your sentence. Seems like you've got nothing but time."

"Time has a funny way of running out while we're busy thinking we're going to get more. You know that." His words are sobering because of how true they are. "Now why don't you stop being such a pussy, and tell me why you look like you just found out your sister died all over again."

"Shit," I chuckle under my breath. "Good to know you still have absolutely no filter or finesse whatsoever."

"Aww, fuck you, kid." His tone is gruff, but affectionate. "If you wanted filters, finesse, or flowery words, you wouldn't have put yourself through the embarrassment of coming back here, and we both know it."

My eyes flit to the officers standing guard by the door. "I suppose that's true enough."

"So let's get on with it then, shall we?"

"It's kind of a long story . . ."

"Did we not just establish that I've got the time?" He tilts his palms up with the query. "Now hurry up and stop wasting it."

Shaking my head at his impatience, I lean forward to tell him why I came.

I tell him about my sudden craving for a cigarette and the way I stopped at the little, forgotten gas station in Georgia with little hope of finding one. I tell him about Smokey, and the way it felt like I could somehow reach back in time to save Amy by saving her. I tell him how every minute I spent with her started to make me feel like she was the one saving me.

"You ran from her, didn't you?" He interjects with a knowing smirk.

"I didn't plan on it!" The words burst out of me defensively.

"Didn't you?" He counters, the light in his eyes as sharp as ever, despite his increasing age. "Wasn't that the whole plan? Save her, so you could feel absolved of your past, and then drop her off . . ." He shrugs his shoulders noncommittally. "Wherever?"

"Yes, but things changed!" The defensive edge is still in my tone, but as soon as the words leave my mouth, I deflate in my seat. That's the first time I ever admitted it out loud. That despite my intentions, things between Smokey and I had changed— evolved beyond my control, and I didn't know what to do about that.

"Things changed, and that scared you?"

"Yes. No. I don't know!" I close my eyes and cover my face with my hands, pushing my palms into my eye sockets. "She lied to me."

I confess. "About her age." When I drop my hands and open my eyes I find him looking at me no differently than before. "Do you understand what I'm getting at, here, Gibbs?"

"Yes, I believe so." The old man nods. "And when you found out, you ran away."

I heave a sigh of frustration. "Do you have to keep phrasing it like that?"

"No filters and flowery words here, boy. We've already covered that." He winks and I do my best to mask my annoyance.

"Can you just help me? Please?" I implore him, and he looks genuinely surprised.

"What can I do?"

"Tell me what to do. Tell me how I can make this right again."

"Son," he pauses to shake his head in what appears to be amusement, but I fail to see anything funny in the situation. "It's just like I told you last time when I caught you licking your wounds and feeling sorry for yourself in the infirmary all that time ago: It's all about forgiveness."

"I do forgive her." I respond quickly.

"That's great. But can you forgive yourself?"

My silence speaks volumes.

Gibbs simply shakes his head. "That's what I thought." The older man leans forward, adjusting himself in his chair like he's about to say something meaningful. "You could always let go of everything that was done to you, but you never could let go of everything you did." He looks at me seriously. "How much longer are you going to go on like this?"

"Like what?" I ask, trying to curb my exasperation.

"Punishing yourself for the sins of your father."

"If I had just stayed–"

"Yeah, yeah, I've heard that song and dance before." He interrupts, waving me off.

"Go to Hell," I spit with venom, but all he does is laugh.

"If only! Then my time here would finally be served." He cackles some more, leaning back in his seat while I sit and stew across from him.

"You aren't like him, son. Trust me." He finally says after a while.

"How do you know?" I don't look at him as I verbalize the fear that has haunted me since I snapped and killed the old man all those years ago.

"Because you didn't do anything to hurt the girl." He says it simply, like it's obvious.

And maybe it is.

"Why don't you go after her?" He asks after we sit in silence for a bit, as if it's the easiest thing in the world.

"Do you think I didn't already try?" I'm not hiding my impatience at all anymore. *"No one from the hotel would tell me anything."*

"And those people at the hotel are all you have to go on? You didn't learn anything else about her while you were busy falling in love?"

"Whoa, hold on there . . . I'm not . . . I can't be . . . " I flounder for the right words of denial, but come up short.

He smiles knowingly at me. *"Sometimes we reject the things that can hurt us the most before they ever get the chance to. Unfortunately, the result of that is,"* he gestures to me across the table from him, *"becoming a lonely, broken man who doesn't recognize love even when he tackles it into the dust himself."*

"Okay, alright, I get it. You've made your point. I . . . have feelings for her." I begrudgingly admit. "If I can forgive her, and can I forgive myself, how do I go about getting her to forgive me? What do I do if I find her? Blow up her life all over again?" I flick my eyes back to the guards as I lower my voice. "You know stalking is a crime, right?"

"Yeah, and so is kidnapping, but that didn't stop you now, did it?"

"Shhh, old man, before you get me thrown back in here with you." I caution, giving the guards some more side-eye as he continues.

"Just be honest with her, son" he looks at me sharply, pointing a gnarled finger at my chest, "And be honest with yourself."

AFTER SPEAKING WITH Gibbs, I spent some time driving aimlessly across the country sorting through all my thoughts and feelings, just trying to get my mind right. I had ample savings to live off of, as expenses for one don't really add up to much when you live alone on the road. Food, gas, and regular truck maintenance are the only major expenses I've ever had.

As time went on, I found myself drawn to Louisiana in a way I couldn't ignore. Even now, two years later, I scan the load boards for jobs, only calling on the ones that will take me through The Crescent City. I can't seem to help myself.

I know it's crazy to think that our paths will ever cross again, but it's like I'm being pulled by some invisible thread. Part of me wants to believe that it must have something to do with her, but then I think of how nuts that sounds. Even still, here I am, rolling into New Orleans once again.

It's still early enough to be dark out, but a few people linger in the streets, either looking for the next party or a safe place to crash. Even bob-tailing without any cargo, it's nearly impossible to find anywhere big enough to park Black Betty on the historic cobblestone streets.

When I find a lot with a few empty spaces together in a row, I carefully maneuver the vehicle into the opening before bedding down to get a few hours of shut-eye. When all I can do is toss and turn, I give up, deciding to burn off the restless energy by going for a walk instead.

The sun has fully risen when I find myself wandering about in the French Quarter, the heat causing the smells of the city to rise along with the temperature, despite the fact that it's nearly Halloween. Considering the general lack of concern exhibited by its patrons, it's little wonder why.

Just a little while ago, I passed by a guy sitting on the sidewalk with his knees drawn up, elbows resting on them, and his pants around his ankles. He casually unwrapped a yellow fast food wrapper while he sat, bare-assed on the pavement, pissing a river into the street between his dirty, bare feet. He looked right at me as he chewed, but his dull expression never wavered. It was as if he committed repulsive acts like that in front of strangers every day. Maybe he does.

I'm suppressing a shiver of revulsion at the very unwanted memory of street-dick when the sound of laughter not far off stops me in my tracks. I swear, I've heard that throaty sound before. Not often, but it was like fucking magic every time I did, healing me in ways I didn't even know I needed. I hold my breath as I turn in circles, frantically searching for the source when another laugh floats to me on the balmy breeze, and my heart stops when I finally locate her.

Less than a hundred yards from me, outside a little French cafe, stands a Liv Tyler look-alike pushing her long, dark hair over one shoulder while she pours hot coffee from an antique silver carafe into the porcelain cup of an older gentleman sitting at a small, white, wrought-iron table. His lips move as he speaks to her, and I watch in rapt fascination as her cheeks tint before her head tips back and she laughs again. Freely, playfully swatting at the old man's shoulder.

Goosebumps break out over my skin as I'm finally able to draw in a full breath, just the sight of her bringing me comfort after all this time. Each beat of my heart rattles my chest like thunder, and I'm distantly concerned that I may be having a heart attack.

I can't believe I actually found her.

Smokey

Despite the pleasant morning working alongside Annette, doing my best to absorb as much of her magical pastry mojo as possible, I can't help the unsettled feeling that lingers with me throughout the morning rush. When the endless barrage of customers dwindles down to a manageable amount of stragglers, I remove my well-used apron and excuse myself for my first break of the day.

"Take the rest of the day and celebrate, *mon cher*." Annette hands me a chocolate croissant and a warm to-go cup with a splash of cream the way she taught me to like. "I think I can manage on my own for the rest of the day, *oui*?"

"*Évidemment*," I respond easily as I gratefully accept her edible offerings. "I just don't feel much like celebrating for some reason." I shrug my shoulders sheepishly, as if I expect her to be disappointed in me. On the contrary, she pulls me in for an affectionate side-hug, kisses my cheek, and says, "You should call Jan. Go have a *tête-à-tête*. Then stop at one of those intriguing little magic shops you love, and buy yourself a gift, hmm? It doesn't have to be a big celebration." She raises a perfectly manicured eyebrow before she nudges me with her hip and walks away to help the customer who just approached the counter.

She's right about calling my therapist. Talking with Jan always makes me feel a little better. More grounded and in control of my memories and the thought patterns they can provoke. After taking a giant bite of the warm, flaky pastry, I take my goodies and head upstairs to shower and make a phone call.

ALREADY FEELING STEADIER just being on my way to Jan's office, I sip at what's left of my tepid to-go coffee while I admire the faded plastic beads that drip from the trees and surrounding power lines. They remind me of the Spanish moss that grows so rampant here, mimicking the long beards of old, wise men, serving as ancient reminders of forgotten parties, and parades long past.

New Orleans is such a mystical place. With its rich history and dark secrets, it's a city steeped in magic and mystery, and I love the way anything feels possible here.

The trolley slows to a stop, and I slide into the short line of passengers ambling towards the front exit. The busy streetcars are one of my favorite things about the city. Even though Annette helped me get my license, I don't really care much for driving. Being in a confined space like that just makes me think of...him.

My heart aches the way it always does when I miss him, and I absentmindedly rub at my chest like I can erase the feeling as I step onto the sidewalk.

The small hairs on the back of my neck prickle to attention, and I find myself glancing around inexplicably, looking for the source of the peculiar feeling. Nothing about my surroundings stands out, so I shake it off and continue across the street to the Hope Healing Center.

It's not as luxe as it sounds. It's not so much a "center," as much as it's just two kind individuals who rent a small space where they provide counseling to individuals without insurance for little to no cost.

If there's one thing I've learned in my two years of freedom, it's that there are far more good people in the world than bad ones, we just have to be brave enough to look for them.

Trust isn't always a trap.

I know this because of people like Grace, Annette, and Jan. Even Jackson, if I'm being honest. Funny how my thoughts keep circling back to him today, reminding me why I'm here.

"Hey, Mave." I greet the receptionist who also happens to be the wife of the other doctor renting the space. "I just called a little bit ago—"

"I remember, dear," she cuts me off good-naturedly. "I'm not that old, yet." She chuckles at my tell-tale blush and offers me a kind smile. "Dr. Greer will be with you in a moment."

"Dr. Greer will be with you right now." Jan appears behind Mave looking more like she's about to tell my fortune than counsel me with her Ivy League credentials. "Come on back," she waves at me while turning on her bare heel with a flourish.

"Thanks, Mave. Say hi to Dave for me." I nod at her as I walk past her desk.

"Will do, honey."

Yes, she and her husband are actually named Mave and Dave, and I've never met a couple more in love in my entire life. They've been together for over forty years already, and they give me so much hope for the future.

Closing the door to Jan's office, I immediately plop down into my favorite green velvet chair. I swear, the deep emerald color embodies the soul of this city. The soft material reminds me of moonlight on the bayou, the wind whispering its secrets to the trees while cicadas sing lullabies to lightning bugs. It's the color of magic.

Jan doesn't sit behind a stodgy desk. Bad feng shui, she claims. How am I supposed to feel compelled to open up and share myself with her if there's a great hunk of separation between us? Instead, she makes herself comfortable on the brown suede couch across from me, her purple painted toes curling and uncurling into the plush fabric beneath her. She doesn't ask me any questions or push me to talk. We sit in companionable silence, appreciating the warm October breeze that blows through the open windows, rustling the leaves of the many plants stashed around the room. Jan has the greenest of thumbs, and her office is an earthy reflection of that. I think that's part of what makes it so peaceful.

"So," I begin, drawing the word out into the silence between us. "It's my birthday today."

"Yes, it is. Happy birthday." She smiles kindly at me. "Do you have any special plans?"

"You mean besides having a pity party with my therapist?" I laugh nervously at my half-joke. Jan's eyes squint a little as she tilts her head the barest amount, but she stays quiet, waiting for me to elaborate on my own. taking a deep breath, I cover my face with my hands, then drop them in my lap as I let it out in a gusty sigh.

"I am now the actual age I lied about being two years ago."

"Ah," she says, nodding her head in understanding. She knows everything that transpired in my former life, but her face gives nothing away now.

"Ah? That's it? You don't have any other spectacular insight you want to add to that?" I ask her in mock exasperation, and the corner of her mouth twitches with the hint of a smile.

"What type of insight were you looking for?" she queries.

"Has anyone ever told you how annoying it is that you only seem to answer questions with *other* questions?" I ask, lifting a sardonic brow.

"Absolutely," she responds without hesitation, causing me to roll my eyes. She huffs out a laugh and readjusts to sit criss-cross applesauce. "I'm supposed to help you find the answers within yourself, Smokey, not just give them to you. *You* have to do the work. I'm just a guide...Like Jesus."

She says the last part with a shrug of her narrow shoulders.

Jan and I have talked at length about religion and spirituality over the last two years, so she knows I won't be offended by her words, but I still can't contain my snort of disbelief.

"Comparing yourself to deities now? Someone has an awfully high opinion of themselves." I say sarcastically, and this time it's her turn to roll her eyes.

"I just mean that whenever you read The Bible, and Jesus asks a question, do you think he was ever actually interested in the answer?" She waits a beat, letting her question sink in before going on. "Or did he just need whoever he was dealing with to be more honest with themselves?"

We sit in comfortable silence for a moment as I ponder her words.

"The goal has always been to encourage you to think for yourself, Smokey. Answering questions, or choosing *not* to answer them," she says with a smirk, "means that you have it within your power to do so. You have the power of choice. You are in control of the direction of your life, no matter what your past has taught you."

"Then why can't I control the way I miss him?"

The question tumbles from my mouth before I even know what I'm saying.

"How long will I carry the absence of him with me? How long will I feel empty like this?"

One after another, I fire the questions at her.

"I've made a good life for myself. I have more than I ever could have imagined, and I've fought for every bit of it, so why does it still feel like something is missing? How much longer do I have to keep fighting for every little piece of myself?"

I look at her through blurry eyes clouded by tears of desperation.

She leans forward, offering me a tissue from the box on the end table beside her.

"Until you have all of them put back exactly where you want them."

Jackson

It was a risky thing to do, getting on the same trolley as her that day. But I couldn't risk letting her out of my sight. Once I had found her, I was reluctant to let the vision of her go again, afraid it wouldn't be real.

When she disappeared into the Hope Healing Center, I stood across the street and immediately looked it up on my phone. It's a little rinky-dink operation providing mental health services to people who probably wouldn't be able to get the help they need otherwise. They're a "pay what you can" kind of facility, even if what you can pay is nothing. It's amazing that they can get away with that in today's economy.

I'm glad she found a good place to help her process all the trauma she has lived through. I can't help but wonder where I rank on that scale. I probably don't even want to know.

I've continued following her since that day, feeding my need to be close to her again, yet staying just far enough on the edges of her life that she never notices. She's looked around a few times as if she can sense someone watching her, but I'm not ready to let her see me. Not yet, at least. But I know, eventually, I'll have to reveal myself to her. I hate to imagine what it would be like if she caught me stalking her after I left her the way I did.

In the past two weeks, I've discovered that she drinks way too much coffee and has a penchant for charms and incense from the varied selection of voodoo shops the city has to offer. She doesn't seem to favor any one location over another, losing herself in whatever oddities are on display in each one.

I know that the owner and store clerk of a chaotic little restaurant called Readers Digest is named Jaime, and that he seems to be very familiar with my little smoke show, as they're on a first-name basis with each other. The place is also part bookstore, but he seems to allow Smokey to treat the numerous overstuffed shelves as her own personal library, never buying anything, just borrowing. I have a love/hate relationship with the way he makes her smile.

I love it when she smiles. It's radiant. She deserves to smile.

I just hate that she smiles at *him*.

My jealousy aside, I'm honestly impressed by who she's become since the last time I saw her. She seems to have grown up so much, but I don't know what else I expected. She didn't wait for me to come back and save her when I left her in that hotel room, and she doesn't need saving now. I thought she needed it back then, and I guess maybe she did at first, but it didn't take her long to figure out how to do it all by herself.

She's found herself here, built a new life. She has a job she seems to enjoy and excel at, friends she can laugh with, even a fricking cat for shit's sake. She has so much to lose now if I try to walk back into her life. And what do I have to offer? An apology and my passenger seat?

I gaze at her as she reads, totally engrossed in whatever world lays open before her as the sultry evening breeze plays with her hair the way I wish I could.

Books may be the only way some people have to escape.

I hear her voice from the past whisper through my mind and wonder what part of her life she's escaping from right now.

A better man would let her go.

I guess I'm not a better man.

Smokey

An angry barrage of foreign curse words floats out from the kitchen, loud enough to be heard over the grinding and hissing of the espresso machine. It's been an insane morning with me overseeing the cafe side of things, while Annette works in the kitchen, preparing the confections and cakes for a Halloween themed wedding we'll be catering later today.

I slide what feels like my millionth to-go cup of *cafe au lait* across the counter toward another satisfied customer before turning to the waiting baskets of fresh beignets. The little service bell on the counter behind me chimes *again,* just as I'm dusting them with powdered sugar.

"Be right with you!" I toss over my shoulder. Turning with the canister in my hand proves to be a mistake when it clatters promptly to the floor as I register who I'm looking at.

White powder coats my old, worn sneakers, and the checkered black and white pattern of the floor around me.

"Hey, Liv," he offers me that familiar smirk through his sexy beard. It's thicker than it used to be, and I hate the way I notice, automatically cataloging all the little changes I can find in his appearance.

"What are you doing here?" I blurt out. He's not even around me for two whole seconds, and I lose my ability to think. Great. *Just breathe,* I hear Jan's comforting voice reminding me that I'm not the same as I once was. I have the tools now to navigate through my anxieties, and the ability to process my emotions without losing myself to them.

I am in control. I repeat the mantra to myself until the heavy, tingling sensation in my palms dissipates.

"Smokey?" I snap back to reality and notice Jackson's face contorted with concern.

"What? What are you doing here?" I ask again, but his expression doesn't change.

"I was in the area and heard good things about the place..." he speaks hesitantly. "I thought I'd come check it out... Do you not remember me saying this just a second ago?" he asks, eyebrows raised.

"No," I respond immediately before quickly correcting myself, "I mean yes, of course I do! I just don't believe you." I cross my arms defensively over my chest. *Nice save, Liv,* I snark at myself, and then roll my eyes internally for using the same nickname in my subconscious that he just used.

"Really? That's funny, since I never lied to *you*." He fires the shot at me, and I feel the impact deep in my chest. My tell-tale cheeks give away my feelings, and Jackson ducks his head sheepishly while running tense fingers through his dark, coppery hair.

Mesmerized by the movement, I notice hints of silver that weren't there two years ago glistening within the strands. It's longer than I remember, too. He takes a deep, grounding breath, and as his chest expands, I can't help but notice how broad he is. Instead of making me feel afraid, the way he dwarfed me always made me feel safe. Protected. Like nothing could get to me as long as he was around. It made his presence addictive, after never having experienced that before.

"I'm sorry." His apology brings me back to the present, and my gaze snaps back up to his. His dark brown eyes are warm and full of sincerity as he speaks. "I didn't mean to attack you. That wasn't fair, and not at all how I intended to start this conversation. Look–" His eyes dart around the crowded cafe, "Can we go somewhere?"

The urge to tell him to fuck off is strong...But the desire to let myself be near him again? That's even stronger. Besides, what are the odds that he would show up just in time for my break?

"Uhmm..." I don't get to say anymore before another blend of profanities spew from the back. "I'd better go check on Annette!" The words leave me in a rush right before I disappear into the kitchen, leaving the mess of unresolved feelings and spilled powdered sugar behind.

I find the woman in question violently banging cake pans over the trash bin, splotches of brown marring her otherwise pristine apron. "Is everything okay?" I inquire, my voice coming out higher and squeakier than usual.

"*Tonnerre m'a écrase!*" She spits as she crosses the kitchen to toss the now empty pans into the sink with an angry clatter. "The delivery driver just called and said due to a scheduling error, he won't be coming to pick up the desserts for the Legasse wedding. Now, I must find another driver at the last minute, with an available truck..." She continues her tirade, weaving sentences out of her own peculiar blend of English and Louisiana Creole about how taking the call caused her to burn a few layers of the cake.

As her outburst winds down, she turns to me, her expression immediately changing as the frustration and annoyance melt from her face.

"*Sa ena*?" She asks suddenly, her brows pinching together as she assesses me.

"He's here," I tell her, as if that explains everything.

"Who is here, *cher*?" she asks in confused amusement as she notices the white powder coating my shoes. The very same ones *he* bought me two years ago, in fact. My sad, sentimental ass couldn't bear to part with them.

"Him. Jackson." I can feel my cheeks growing hot all over again.

"*Vré?*" she asks in disbelief, her eyebrows disappearing into her hairline. "*Pou kisa?*"

"Yes, really!" I respond, trying not to acknowledge the nerves running through me. "And I'm not completely sure why...I think he just wants to talk. He asked if we could go somewhere." She consults the clock on the stove. "You have the time. Do you want to talk to him?" I chew on my lip as I consider the possibility of *not* talking to him.

"I don't know..." I finally say, even though I *do* know. Of course I want to talk to him. I've missed him for two years. But what does one say to the man who snatched them from Hell, introduced them to Heaven, and then left them behind in purgatory?

"Do you think the cake could fit in his truck?" she asks suddenly, her eyes bright with inspiration as she breezes past me, pulling me from my intrusive thoughts.

"Huh? No, Annette. Wait!" I sputter after her in shock.

We both stop short in the entrance from the kitchen as we watch Jackson sweep up what's left of the mess I made earlier, and dump the contents into the trash can under the counter.

"Did someone have an accident?" she asks with another signature eyebrow raise as she looks back down at my feet. Her question draws his attention to us standing behind him, and as always, my cheeks color with uncertainty when our gazes meet.

"You didn't have to do that," I mumble as I look down at my still powdered shoes.

"I know," he says easily, placing the little hand broom and dustpan combo back under the counter where he found them.

"You must be Jackson." Annette addresses him, giving him a lingering once-over.

"I must be," he confirms for her. "And you are?"

"Wondering if you still have your truck," she tells him frankly.

"Annette!" I scold, embarrassed. "I'm so sorry for her rudeness, but it will probably happen again. She has no boundaries." I give my friend a look of complete exasperation.

"Sure, I still have my truck. Why do you ask?" He responds to Annette without taking his eyes off me. Goosebumps break out all over my body as I recall the time we spent together in that very truck. I'm oddly comforted that he still has it.

"How much cake do you think it will hold?"

"Do what?"

She finally succeeds in getting his attention, confusion written plainly all over his face when he turns to her.

"Annette..." I smile nervously as I try to stop my friend from manipulating him into helping us this evening. I'm not sure I can handle that.

"Cake," she says matter-of-factly to him as if it's an obvious explanation. "Can we fit some in your truck or not?"

"Uhmm..." He looks back to me for guidance.

"We have a wedding to cater this evening, and our regular delivery service just canceled due to some sort of scheduling conflict." I shrug my shoulders as if to say, "What can you do?"

"Ah," he says in understanding.

"So do you have room for cake or not?" Annette presses impatiently.

"Annette..." I say her name again, as if it's helping in some way.

"Sure," Jackson answers, cutting off any chance I had at an argument. "Everyone has room for cake, don't they?" he asks before flashing that damn smirk at Annette as he winks in my direction.

Jackson

"Oui, exactly!" Annette claps her hands together in obvious excitement. Smokey, however, looks less than thrilled by my agreement to help.

"Do you even know what you're getting into?" she asks, appearing amused at my expense as she folds her arms across her chest.

"Yeah, I'm helping my...a friend." I almost choke on the word as I shove my hands into my pockets so that I won't feel so tempted to touch her. *My little smoke show* is what I almost just said, but I have to remember that she doesn't belong to me. I can't just revert back to how I treated her in the past. That would negate all of the healing she's accomplished since then, and I don't ever want to take that from her. Just because every cell in my body tells me to claim her, doesn't mean that she wants to be mine. After everything she's been through, what she wants matters. It's fucking paramount, in fact. It has to be her choice. Always.

"What exactly do you know about hauling around several hundred pounds of French pastry in the Louisiana heat?" Her question brings me back to the here and now, where she's raising a challenging eyebrow at me. Thankfully, I'm saved from having to pull something clever out of my ass when Annette speaks for me.

"Ah, but he can learn! Just like you did, *non*?" She and Smokey share a look before Annette turns back to me. "You," she points a finger in my direction, "follow me, and I'll show you what needs to be done first. Then you can show me your truck and we can discuss cleaning, sanitizing, and cooling. Smokey..." She pauses to glance at the ornate iron clock on the wall, "Go on break."

And with that, she grabs my forearm in her deceptively strong hand, pulling me along behind her.

Smokey

Despite my reluctance, I can feel myself softening towards Jackson. Again. Even Annette seems to be falling prey to his easy charm.

I glance over at her while she animatedly inspects the refrigerated truck Jackson rented in lieu of trying to prep his own for transporting high-quality baked goods. It's obvious he did some research about it, and her delight is contagious, even as hornets swarm in my stomach at the thought of sharing space with him again.

La Petite Mort has been closed since the end of the morning rush on account of the wedding we're about to cater, and apparently Jackson has volunteered to stay for the duration and help with the whole thing.

I wish I knew what his motives were.

Why is he here now, after all this time? Am I strong enough to be strictly professional with him? Do I want to be? Is there another option? Static begins to fill my ears as the questions run rampant through my mind. *Ground yourself, Smokey*. Jan's voice is in my head again, interrupting my spiral with one of the coping mechanisms she taught me.

Breathing in deep through my nose, I close my eyes and concentrate on something I can smell; *rich coffee, fried dough, and the faintest hint of sugared citrus lingering in the air.* Then I release the air slowly through my mouth.

Drawing in another, I concentrate on what I can hear; *Jackson's deep, soothing baritone drawl, followed by Annette's tinkling laughter, and the sound of their footsteps as they walk back this way.* My lips twitch in a small, reluctant smile as I release the second breath.

Eyes still closed, I inhale once more while focusing on something tangible I can feel; *the solid ground beneath my feet, strands of loose hair brushing against my neck and shoulders from the messy bun I piled on top of my head, Jackson's curious, burning gaze...* My eyes snap open and connect directly with his.

He stands about three feet away, staring at me like he's trying to see *through* me. I send up a quick prayer that he can't, as I square my shoulders and clear my throat. I'd be mortified if he knew how strongly his presence still affects me. It's like I've slipped back in time, and I'm still just a lost and broken girl, desperately clinging to the illusion of safety and security when he's around.

"Can I give you a hand?" His voice is both a balm and an affliction. It heals me, even as it hurts.

"Uhmm, yeah..." I flounder amidst the sea of my emotions. "All of these boxes need to go," I gesture weakly towards the countertops ladened with the stacks of bakery boxes I just finished labeling and organizing into neat rows. "But we won't actually need you until it's time to move the cake." I flick my eyes towards him, then away again.

"Oh yeah? Are you saying you don't need me right now?" He smiles easily as he gently lifts a stack of boxes into his arms.

While his tone is innocent, the question hits me directly in the feels, and I can't stop my defensive response.

"No, Jackson." I meet his playful look with a somber one of my own. "I don't."

I push away from the counter then, desperate to put space between us so I can breathe again.

I'm not sure what has me more shook up right now, the fact that I just told the man I've been pining after that I don't need him, or the sudden realization that it's true.

Jackson

N o *Jackson. I don't.*

No matter how hard I try, I can't stop hearing those words and picturing the way her face looked when she said them. I was only teasing her before, but her ominous response sent chills through me. I wanted to go after her, but the way she spoke was so...final. I grip the cardboard tighter in my hands as I continue to cart boxes to the truck I rented just for this purpose while I try to convince myself that I still stand a chance.

I'm constantly caught off guard by how much she's changed in the last two years. She's not as soft as she used to be. Not as malleable. Not as forgiving. Despite myself, I can't stop the edges of my mouth from curling into a satisfied smile as I contemplate her level response.

She doesn't need me? Good.

I want her to trust herself and know how capable she is.

It's going to take some time for her to adjust to the idea of me again. For her to realize that I'm not here to take anything from her...or to take her away from anything, as it were.

Not this time.

I sneak a glance her way as we pass by each other, her arms so full of white pastry boxes she can barely see over them. She's so perfect to look at it actually pains me, but it hurts more if I look away.

So I don't.

I watch her plump, delectable ass as she climbs into the truck, the thick muscles in her thighs flexing with the motion. The desire to sink my teeth into her flesh, to taste the warm coppery flow of her blood again overwhelms me, and I have to force my gaze away before I do something reckless.

I had thought Smokey was just being snarky when she referenced several hundred pounds of pastry earlier, but It definitely feels like we have carried that many boxes. None of that compares to the pumpkin, caramel, and dark chocolate monstrosity the three of us had to balance on a cake board while we took coordinated baby steps towards the idling vehicle, though.

I'm actually still in awe of the sheer strength and finesse I witnessed the two women display as they carefully installed the wedding cake into its designated place in the back of the truck. Other than taking the brunt of the weight for a moment when they needed to shift around me, I barely helped at all. It's a little humbling to realize what Smokey said before is completely true.

She doesn't seem to need me at all.

I'm dedicated to changing that, though. It won't be an easy feat with the way she's avoiding me right now, but that's alright. I know there's still *something* between us. Otherwise she wouldn't be trying so hard to act like there isn't. And that's all the hope I need.

"That's everything." Annette announces as she shuts and locks the back doors, sealing all the confectionary creations into the cool, refrigerated air.

"Good, we need to get on the road in the next twenty minutes or we're going to be late. Annette, where are the keys?" Smokey checks her watch while she speaks before holding out her palm.

"I have them here," the other woman answers, patting her apron pocket.

"Well, can I have them?" Smokey counters with an eyebrow raise.

"*Non,* I need you to ride with Jackson, *cher.* Someone needs to keep an eye on the cake as it travels, you know that." Smokey flicks her eyes to me, then quickly away again. Was that a spark of annoyance I saw? Or was it just uncertainty?

"No, Annette, we talked about this." Her voice carries an edge now, even though she's obviously trying to keep her cool. "*You* were going to ride with Jackson, and *I* was going to follow behind in your car. Remember?" She offers a tight smile in my direction as if it will cover up the fact she doesn't want to be alone with me.

"*Oui*, I remember. But this arrangement makes more sense."

"Oh, does it?" Smokey's voice drips with uncontained sarcasm as she crosses her arms in front of her. "Please enlighten me then."

Yeah, I'd say it's a pretty sure bet that she's annoyed right now.

Annette responds in a language I don't understand, which has Smokey throwing her hands up and rolling her eyes.

"Oh my God, if it will make you shut up and stop pushing then fine! We'll do it your way. But you and I are going to talk about this later–in *English*." She points a stern finger at the grinning Annette before spinning on her heel and getting into the passenger side of the truck. She doesn't even spare me a second glance.

"What are you so happy about?" I ask the other woman.

"I don't know what you mean." She replies innocently before sauntering off to her car.

If I didn't know any better, I might start to think that Annette is actually rooting for me.

Smokey

The ride to the venue was the most excruciating twenty-seven minutes of my life. I'm pretty sure I counted every second, praying that he wouldn't want to talk...while also praying that he would.

That's the problem isn't it? I can't ever seem to figure out what I'm feeling whenever he's around, and that's as confusing as it is frustrating. It's also exhausting.

Placing my hands on the small of my back, I attempt to stretch and loosen the muscles that are all knotted there. A group of men congregated at the bar obviously appreciate the way the action arches my spine, unintentionally pushing my breasts out, because one of them points at me just before miming the universal symbol for motor boating. I stifle a sigh as I look away, and like magnets, my eyes are drawn to the end of the table where Annette teaches Jackson how to plate the many different delights she prepared for the occasion.

I can't help but laugh at the way she slaps his hands away whenever he makes a mistake, firmly correcting him before allowing him to try again.

"*Non!* What is this? What are these spaghetti arms?" She comically mocks his form before wiping the plate clean with the rag that stays slung over her shoulder. "Watch again! You must have strong arms. Be steadfast. Be quick, and be sure of yourself." She flawlessly demonstrates her technique before offering the spoon back to him. Jackson's eyebrows draw together in determination as he dips the implement back into the caramel sauce once more. This time, he swipes it across the delicate china with swift, yet gentle precision, earning a pleased, "*Trè bon!*" from Annette as she claps her hands in encouragement.

He looks up suddenly, and catches me watching him. I can feel the tell-tale heat rising in my cheeks at being caught, but I find it impossible to look away. His eyes shine bright with the pure, unadulterated joy of accomplishment, while an unexpectedly shy smile curves his lips, and my breath catches at the sight.

Have I ever seen Jackson happy like this? So open and unguarded? So *vulnerable*? The man I remember was thoroughly stuck in the past, but the one I see now? He looks capable of having a future...*a future with me.*

The thought makes my stomach lurch and heart pound, allowing me to look away and break the spell he put me under. I'm not sure if something like that is actually possible, or if it's even something I should want. I hate how indecisive and unsure I've become since his reappearance in my life.

"Excuse me, miss? I couldn't help but wonder if it hurt?" One of the men from the bar is standing in front of me and it takes me a moment to process his strange question.

"I'm sorry, what? Did what hurt?" I'm sure confusion is as plain on my face as it is in my tone.

"When you fell from Heaven," he says with what I'm sure he thinks is a charming wink. You'd think such a smartly dressed man would have a better pick-up line than that.

"Uhmm…" I'm unsure of how to respond when I feel the peculiar weight of someone else's eyes on me. Even without looking, I know that they're *his*. There's a familiarity to the way they burn along my skin, igniting something inside me that only he knows how to reach.

But I don't have to let *him* know that.

Jackson

I watch her as she leans into the sharply dressed gentleman who just approached the dessert table, laughing at whatever line he just hit her with. Sure, maybe she's just being nice. Friendly. She represents a business here after all. But then she pulls that plush bottom lip of hers between her teeth, biting it as she looks down, then back up at him through her long, dark lashes.

The celebratory party noise fades out around me, replaced by the loud rush of blood echoing in my ears. Then, because I'm watching every little move she makes so, so closely, I notice the almost imperceptible way her blue eyes cut to mine, as she allows his hand to graze hers as she passes one of the plates I worked so hard on to him.

Oh, I see. My Little Smoke Show still likes to play with fire.

Relief races through me at the thought, and I suck in a deep breath from the welcome feeling. Perhaps there's more hope for us than I thought.

Smokey

Surprisingly, the event passes in a blur, but it's probably because I spent the entire evening trying to evade being left alone with Jackson for any real measure of time. I flirted with other men I'm not even interested in just to keep him at arm's length, and now I'm kind of mad at myself for letting him have such a negative effect on my behavior. He makes me act like someone I'm not, and I don't like feeling as though I don't have a grip on my own actions or emotions when he's around. I'm not a child anymore, and I resent being knocked backwards into the mental space where I act like one.

"Did I do something?" His southern drawl sounds languidly from behind me as I slam the doors to the delivery truck closed. All of the equipment is already packed back up, ready to be hauled back to *La Petite Mort* where Annette and I will probably spend the rest of our night cleaning until the wee hours of the morning.

"Is that a joke?" I ask sarcastically, even though I was just telling myself how I wasn't going to act like a child around him anymore.

"Do I look like I'm joking?" he counters, and I stop to actually assess him head-on, not just in quick glimpses and stolen side-glances. He's heart-poundingly handsome, and looking at him does something to me that's hard to explain.

His facial hair is longer and a little more unkempt than I remember it. It was probably the highlight of my night when Annette asked him to tie it up in a hairnet, claiming it was a potential health hazard. It wasn't actually necessary for the event, but she tried to help me attain a small, comical piece of revenge nonetheless. Until he enthusiastically accepted the embarrassing challenge with a gleam in his eye, as if he knew exactly what we were up to and was willing to play the game.

He looks so adorable standing in front of me now, his beard still ensnared by the elastic mesh, and a sexy man-bun on top of his head. It's all I can do to keep from cracking a cheesy smile.

"You look a little like Annette's punchline right now, yeah." I gesture to his beard with an amused smirk, and he rolls his eyes, reaching up to untangle the fine netting from his face. My mouth goes dry watching the deft way his thick fingers work, and I flounder for anything to say to distract myself from the rogue coil of desire tightening in my lower belly.

"You did well tonight," I say.

The flattery sounds sudden and insincere, but it's true. He worked mostly behind the scenes, under the careful eye of Annette, who tends to exchange her easy-going, *laissez-faire* attitude for a German drill sergeant personality during these types of public business ventures. If I think about it too long, I could almost feel sorry for him. *Almost.*

"Seriously, though," he presses, ignoring my praise. His dark, liquid eyes full of some unnamed emotion. "Did I do something to upset you?" The question is fair, but it pulls a trigger that's been cocked ever since he reappeared in my life a few hours ago.

"No, of course not, Jackson. Why would being abandoned in the middle of nowhere with nothing and no one be upsetting?" I snap, wearily shoving my hands into the large pockets of my open chef's jacket, already exhausted by this confrontation. His gaze tracks the movement, snagging on the way my raspberry-colored silk blouse pulls tight across my chest beneath the stiff white linen. I have the buttons undone now that the party is winding down, trying to catch a hint of the evening breeze that kisses my skin every so often.

"How did you even find me?" My tone is indifferent, disguising the immense emotional turmoil I feel within.

"It wasn't hard to guess where you would end up after everything you told me." He shrugs, and I nod my head in agreement and understanding, but remain silently aloof.

"Do you know what it was like for me? Finding out your real age like that?" The anguish in his voice cuts through the tension between us like a knife, flaying me open, and I have to close my eyes to hide the pain from him. My voice is choked with barely contained emotion whenever I speak, but he passionately cuts me off.

"I'm sorry, Jackson. I never should have lied to you…"

"No, damn it, I don't want you to apologize to me, okay? You didn't do anything wrong." He lets out a sigh that ruffles the hair on top of my head.

"…O-Okay?" The confusion is evident in my voice as I blink my watery eyes open in surprise.

I hadn't realized he had gotten so close, but now that I'm aware of his proximity, it's a little hard to focus on the conversation. I can feel his body heat radiating towards me, wrapping the smell of tobacco around my senses, so that it takes all of my willpower not to lean further into him as he continues to whisper brokenly to me.

"I get why you lied, Smokey. This world gave you no reason to trust anybody, least of all a stranger like me. I just don't know why you let me...Why you let things go so far. I would have stopped." He looks me dead in the eye, the sincerity of his words palpable between us as he finishes.

"I know." The words are barely audible. I've wondered that myself and talked about it extensively in therapy with Jan. "I think..." I halt myself before uttering the words I'm just learning to accept myself. His eyes search my face as he waits patiently for me to go on. "I think that's exactly why I let it happen. Because for the first time ever...I was the one with all the power." My words tremble, but I don't look away from him as I offer my truth. "And I couldn't say no to that. To *finally* being the one in control. It was almost as good as the orgasms you gave me." I look away from him as hot nerves prickle in my cheeks, but when his hand caresses the side of my face, I can't keep my gaze from meeting his.

"You don't have to be ashamed, Smokey. I've been yours to command ever since. It just took some time for me to figure that out."

Jackson

I stare back at her as she gapes at me, wondering if she knows that I just handed her my heart.

I didn't know it until I saw her again, but I don't ever want to go another day without her in my life. One glimpse of her is all it took for the muscle in my chest to feel like it was being electrocuted and brought back to life like Frankenstein's monster. An overwhelming sense of *MINE* roars through me whenever she's near, and I don't know how to ignore that. What's more is, I don't *want* to ignore it. There is only one person who could make me walk away from her for good, and she still hasn't said anything in response to my earlier statement.

"Smokey?" I attempt to brush a wayward strand of dark hair from her face, but she takes a few steps back, batting my hand away as she snaps out of her daze.

"We can't do this, Jackson." She strides further away, putting distance between us entirely too fast. Ice fills my veins at her tone, but I work to conceal it.

"We can't do what, Smoke Show?" I follow behind her, taking long strides to catch up.

"Don't call me that," she snaps back over her shoulder.

"Why not?"

"Because I'm not that girl anymore!" The words explode from her mouth as she whirls on me, causing her messy bun to come loose from its precarious position atop her head. The dark tresses tumble down her back in what seems like slow motion as she aims those beautiful orbs of blue fire at me, making her look every bit like a fierce goddess in the moonlight. She points a demanding little finger in my direction, underscoring her words as she advances on me.

"I'm not your '*Liv*,' or your '*Little Smoke Show*!' That girl barely existed as anything more than a broken, messed-up piece of your past. You didn't waste time leaving her behind, and neither did I."

She's right in front of me now, poking me in the chest as hers heaves beneath the deep red color of her blouse. "I'm not your ticket into Heaven anymore, okay? You can't wash your sins clean by playing savior to mine." She takes a deep breath, squaring her shoulders and shaking her loose hair back before looking at me proudly. "I learned to save myself. So maybe you should just—"

She stops talking abruptly, but it's only because I've sealed my mouth firmly over hers.

God, she tastes good. Rich and sweet, like the sugary confections we peddled here this evening. The way she melts in my arms is even better, though. Like she knows she belongs in my embrace.

She kisses me back with equal enthusiasm, moaning into my mouth as I massage her tongue with my own. Greedily I swallow up all her little sounds, grabbing handfuls of her firm, round ass, boosting her up, encouraging her to wrap her legs around my waist. Once she's clinging to me like a vine, I pin her body between mine and the side of the truck, seeking and applying pressure where we both want it most. She moans some more as she arches into me, trying to get closer still. I want to consume her. I want her to consume me. I want to—

"Ahem." Annette clears her throat from somewhere behind us causing us to jump apart like two guilty teenagers. I glance over at Smokey, but she avoids my gaze, busying herself by doing up the buttons on her thick white chef's coat. I can already tell she's rebuilding her defenses, shoring up the places that were weak before, so that something like this doesn't happen again.

"I don't mean to interrupt, but—" Annette starts, but Smokey doesn't let her finish.

"It's fine. We need to get back anyway so we can finish cleaning up." Then she turns on her heel and walks off, leaving Annette and me behind in a stilted, awkward silence.

"Do you think she'll ever be able to forgive me?" I ask, afraid to hope for an answer. The one that comes doesn't exactly make me feel better, though.

"You threaten everything she's worked hard for ever since she found her way here," Annette says in her delicately accented voice. "You send her back in time to a place where she has no control over who, or even what she is, to the people who were supposed to care for her the most." I feel myself deflate beneath the weight of her words. "But you also take her back to the very first time she felt safe enough to trust herself." She shrugs her shoulders as if to say it could go either way, and mine re-expand with a hopeful breath.

"So what do I do? How do I make her feel safe again?" I ask, sounding more than a little desperate. She eyes me seriously for a moment.

"Show her she is. Then allow her some time to feel it." With a gentle smile and a head tilt, she adds, "See you back at *La Petite* to drop off the truck? You can pick it up and return it in the morning."

"Yeah, just leave the keys in it, and I'll pick it up before you guys even open tomorrow."

"*La vache!* You want it should get stolen?" Her eyebrows are in her hairline as she looks at me in shocked disbelief. Before I can even form a response, she goes on matter-of-factly,

"You will come early for breakfast, and one of us will give you the key."

Since I became very familiar with this totalitarian version of her tonight, I know there's no room here for argument. This Annette may very well cut out my tongue for daring to disagree with her.

"Alright, sure. Yeah. If you insist," I acquiesce easily, and she nods once in satisfaction before leaving me alone in the parking lot.

Smokey

Jackson didn't try to follow me. He didn't even try to talk to me again to apologize, or anything at all. Not that I'm complaining.

Or Am I?

Before Annette caught us basically sucking each other's faces off while I was blissfully grinding myself on his erection, I definitely didn't think I wanted him around. I wanted space. Lots and lots of space. Because he overrides my senses, and I can't think whenever he's near me. But now that I know how close he is, I hate that he's not here right now.

What the actual fuck is wrong with me?

"Yoo-hoo, Earth to Smokey."

"Huh?" I startle when Annette waves a hand in front of my face, splashing myself with cold, soapy water.

"You've been scrubbing that for the last fifteen minutes." She gestures to the small, copper sauce pot in my pruny hands.

"Oh," I respond lamely. I'm so tired of thinking. And cleaning. I'm just so tired.

"Come on. There are hardly any dishes left, and everything else can be put away later. Let's go upstairs, find something to eat that isn't made of sugar, and then get some rest before we have to brew coffee for what seems like all of New Orleans in a few hours, hmm?" She holds a hand out to me, and I waste no time draining the sink, untying my apron, and walking toward her, allowing her to pull me into an affectionate side hug.

"Do you want to talk about it?" She sounds curious. I consider my answer as I lean into her while we walk, her arm still slung over my shoulders.

"Not really." I sulk.

"Well. Just listen then, because I do." I roll my eyes and pull away from her in front of the staircase that ascends to our apartment. "*Mon ami,*" she starts, cupping my face lovingly in her hands. "Don't let the hate, fear, and uncertainty of your past steal the love, excitement, and joy of your present. You are safe now. No one is taking anything from you." My bottom lip begins to tremble as she speaks to me in earnest. "But consider, perhaps, that you still have something to gain from letting someone else in...from letting them love you."

"I let you in, and you love me," I choke out.

"*Oui,* that's exactly my point, *cher!*" She kisses my temple.

"But I let him in before, and he left me behind." I whine as I dissolve into a mess of tears right there at the foot of the stairs.

Annette holds me, rocking me back and forth, whispering words of comfort until I'm able to breathe without crying. She brushes tear-wet strands of hair from my face as she measures her next words.

"You did not truly let him in, *mon amour*. Not if you felt you had to lie."

I neither confirm nor deny her words, but they follow me up the stairs anyway.

Uncomfortable with the truth they hold and ready to escape reality, I excuse myself from sharing a quick meal together and take myself to bed. Maybe everything will be easier to face once I've had a chance to sleep on it.

I SLEPT LIKE THE DEAD, which is unusual. I'm not even sure I moved once my head hit the pillow. I definitely needed to recharge after the riot of emotions yesterday, but it's still rare for me to sleep through the night on any occasion. It felt like I had just closed my eyes when suddenly the alarm was going off, a riff of smooth jazz ripping me from the comforting bosom of sleep. Too grungy from yesterday's work to hit snooze and skip a shower, I groan as I haul my heavy limbs from the bed and drag them into the bathroom.

I don't mind being awake so much once I'm under the warm spray of water, letting it wash away the tension I carried around after Jackson bulldozed his way back into my life. In the aftermath, I can recognize that I was glad to see him, but that instantaneous spark of excitement also scared the shit out of me. And that pissed me off.

For some reason, I had myself convinced that it was wrong for us to want to be together. As if what we did...what I allowed him to do...was truly so terrible. He may have overreacted, but if I've grown at all, shouldn't I be able to acknowledge and at least try to understand his feelings too? He was already so conscious of our age difference because of what happened to his sister. He gave me every opportunity to tell him to stop or tell him the truth. Instead, I took his choice and helped make him feel like even more of a criminal.

In a way, it's like I took advantage of *him*. He didn't even have the option to consent to what was happening because he didn't *know*. And when I look at it like that, I don't blame him for his panic. Sure, he said some hurtful things when he left, but he was hurt, too. How's that saying go? Hurt people, hurt people. But here he's sought me out after all this time so that he could tell me to my face that he was wrong. Not me...*him*. Doesn't that count for something? And if I'm not that girl anymore, as I so proudly proclaimed, shouldn't I be able to admit to myself that the loss of control I feel whenever I'm with him, are also the moments when I trust myself the most?

Can it really be that easy?

I smile to myself as lavender vanilla sugar scrub runs down the drain, along with my misgivings.

I'm the one in control, aren't I?

Jackson

As I approach the cafe, I mentally repeat the two main directives I gave myself last night while I was waiting for sleep to find me: Keep your hands to yourself, and give her some space to process her emotions.

Annette said to show her that she's safe. That means backing off and letting her get used to the idea of me again. *Before* I start playing love ballads on a boombox outside her bedroom window.

The smells of strong coffee and fresh baked bread permeate the air the closer I get to *La Petite Morte*, and my stomach growls, but it isn't the food here that I fantasize about eating.

As if I conjured her with my thoughts, the object of my obsession appears through the window carrying a large, silver tray of assorted pastries just as I come up to the front door. I take a moment to watch her carefully place each one on the appropriate shelf of the glass display case. Absorbed in her task, I watch her pink tongue poke out between her lips, and my dick jumps involuntarily like it's registering a core memory. As if she's got some sort of radar for it, her eyes suddenly flick up to meet mine through the glass. Then she smiles, and it's radiant, which does nothing to help the growing situation in my pants. But *fuck*, it feels like water for my thirsty soul. I surreptitiously glance behind me for a second to confirm it's really me she's beaming at, and the relief that floods me when there isn't anyone else standing around is unreal.

My attempt to pull open the door is stunted when it doesn't budge, and the pleasant expression on her face only grows as she abandons the now-empty tray on the counter, rounding it to come and unlock it for me. My heart thuds so hard in my chest that I feel lightheaded from the force of it.

The last time I saw her, she didn't seem very happy with me. She definitely wanted me. There's no denying that. She was as helpless to stop what happened between us last night as I was. But it didn't take some sort of genius to read her body language and figure out that she didn't want it to happen again. It's a little hard to reconcile the tense, guarded woman from last night with the cheerful, relaxed one in front of me now. It leaves me feeling slightly off balance, so I don't say anything as I slide past her when she opens the door.

Once inside, I allow her to lead the conversation, letting her have control, as it were. Because she does. She isn't comfortable wielding it over someone other than herself yet, but I very much look forward to teaching her how.

That train of thought isn't doing me any favors, and I take the opportunity to subtly readjust my cock while she's still turned around re-locking the door since they don't open for another half-hour.

"You look like shit," she comments casually as she walks by, and I can't help the startled chuckle that escapes.

"Gee, thanks, Liv," I respond, and immediately regret it when her shoulders go up defensively around her ears like she just heard the worst sound in the world. "I'm sorry, I didn't mean to call you that, I swear. It just kind of slipped out." I shrug my shoulders apologetically. "Old habits and all that."

She recovers quickly, shaking it off with a simple, "No problem," as she walks back around the counter to retrieve her empty tray. "I'd offer to get you some coffee, but I know you wouldn't drink it." She shrugs her shoulders with a wry smile.

"I would if you wanted me too." I respond without hesitation while she looks at me like she's trying to figure me out.

"What does that even mean, Jackson?"

"It means I'll do whatever you want."

She fidgets with the tray in her hands, but her measured gaze doesn't leave mine.

"What if I want you to leave?"

The inflection of her voice gives nothing away, and I have to fight against the wave of revulsion that threatens to overtake me.

"Then I guess I'm gone."

I do my best to hide the disappointment in my tone.

"And if I...if I want you to stay?"

My heart beats faster.

"Then I'll stay."

I take a step closer and her head tilts back, keeping eye contact with me.

"For how long?"

There's uncertainty in her eyes.

"As long as it takes."

I take another step, and though she pulls herself up straighter, she makes no move to retreat.

"Why should I believe you?"

Her voice is stronger now, and more than a little demanding. I can't help but admire the way she stands her ground, so different from the girl I used to know.

"Because even when I tried to walk away from you, I still wound up here."

I stop right in front of her, close enough to feel the warmth of her skin and smell the soothing lavender scent of her body wash. I'm tempted to touch her, but I refrain, wanting the choice to be entirely hers. "I tried so hard to forgive myself for what happened between us, Smokey, only to realize that I'm not really sorry at all." I swallow hard as I finally admit the truth to both of us. "Maybe it wasn't right, but who gets to say if it is or isn't? Life doesn't come with a rule book. Maybe we were just doing the best we could to cope with a difficult situation...two fucked up individuals seeking comfort amidst the chaos...but what if it was more than that?" I look at her earnestly, begging her with my eyes to understand.

"What do you mean?"

It's barely a whisper.

"I'm talking about fate."

I feel a little like a fool when I say it out loud, but the goosebumps I can see breaking out on her arms let me know she feels the same. "I was meant to find you that day, Smokey. Not so I could save *you*, but so you could save *me*." She looks at me like I've lost my mind, but I continue anyway. "I didn't know how to let go of the past until I had to confront losing my future...losing you." She swallows thickly as tears fill her eyes, but she doesn't look away. "I can't promise you that I'll always do the right thing..." She snorts as if that's the understatement of the century and I suppress the smile that wants to spread across my face. "...But I can promise that I'm not going anywhere. Not unless you're coming with me."

"What about your job?" She asks, her voice full of concern.

"I have it on good authority that you're in need of a delivery driver." I offer her a crooked smile, while her eyes bounce back and forth between mine as if she's trying to find the truth in them.

"Will driving a pastry truck be enough for you?"

I don't even have to think about my answer.

"As long as you're still in the truck with me."

After a moment of consideration, she takes a slow step forward, closing the distance between us.

"Well then, I guess you got the job," she says against my lips just before I claim her mouth in a scorching kiss.

Smokey

I t's been six months now, and true to his word, Jackson hasn't gone anywhere. Sometimes I can't believe he's still here, but every day that he is, I feel myself trusting him a little more, opening up to him like a flower in the hot, Louisiana sunshine.

It hasn't all been rainbows and roses, though. Within the first week of our reconciliation we ended up getting into it over his surprise stalking habits.

Jackson had asked me to show him all of my favorite places in New Orleans, so after having our fortunes read by the lovely Madam Simone, I dragged him through the city on several haunted tours before we hopped from one wonderfully odd novelty shop to the next, until we finally made it to my preferred little bookstore and restaurant combo.

"So the way it's supposed to work," I explained as we approached the eclectic looking establishment, "is we go into the bookstore side, browse until we pick some things we like, then we'll take them back to our table and read while we enjoy a nice dinner. Whenever it's time to pay, the books will already be included on the bill."

I beamed up at him, only to find him considering me with a strange expression on his face. "What?" I couldn't help the curiosity burning me up from the inside out.

"I've never seen you buy anything from here, that's all."

"What do you mean you've never *seen* me buy anything from here? I thought this was your first time?"

I crossed my arms over my chest and raised an inquisitive brow when I caught his wince. Then he shook his head in resignation and rubbed the back of his neck as he sighed.

"Alright, you got me. I followed you around for a little while when I first found you–"

"What the hell? For how long?" I interrupted, practically shouting in the middle of the sidewalk.

"Just for a little while–"

"Why? Why would you do that?" I cut him off again as I tried to make sense of the new revelation.

"I guess I just...wanted to get to know you. Who you had become." His shoulders moved up and down as he took a deep breath. "I needed to get my fill of you...just in case you told me to get lost." He offered me a small, weak smile as he lifted his hands, palms up, and then let them drop back to his sides. "That's it. I just...I needed to see you and be near you while I worked up the courage to approach you...while I decided if I even should."

"Why seek me out if you weren't even sure you were going to speak to me?"

"Don't you get it yet, Smoke Show?" He tucked a loose curl behind my ear, caressing my jawline with his thumb before withdrawing his hand. "I had no choice. I couldn't have stopped myself from finding you if I had wanted to. We're connected somehow. Even if I can't quite explain it. I just had to be sure I had something to offer you before I blew up your life again."

"And what exactly are you offering me?"

His answering smile stole my breath.

"Everything."

Shortly after that, we bumped into Jaime, a friendly acquaintance of mine and the current owner of Reader's Digest. Things between the two men were noticeably tense, but everything seemed to be going fine until I laughed at something the smaller man said. Jackson actually growled at him before pulling me close, marking his territory like some sort of latent caveman response. Jaime politely excused himself after the awkward interaction, leaving me to gawk at Jackson's unusual behavior.

He explained that he selfishly wanted to be the source of all my joy, and seeing me light up under another man's attention was unacceptable. I was as touched as I was annoyed when I told him how unfair and unrealistic that was.

In the end, Jackson promised to control his possessive urges whenever I'm obviously enjoying something. He assured me that he never wanted to police the amount of pleasure I'm allowed to find in the world, and ever since then, seems to have found a space where he can just be happy that I'm happy. In fact, he often appears to find a perverse amount of pride in finding new things to experience just so he can see the way delight plays over my face.

Like tonight, he's taking me somewhere he's sure I've never been. He even took me out shopping for a new dress just for the occasion. As I smooth the clinging material over my abdomen again, I look at my reflection and can't help but wonder if it's a bit much. The candy red fabric is form-fitting and eye-catching, with diamond shaped cutouts on either side that come all the way down to my hips, before parting in a slit that comes midway up my right thigh. It's the kind of dress that says, "I'm a bad bitch," and I'm not entirely sure if that's true.

A low whistle sounds behind me, and I meet Jackson's warm, appreciative eyes in the mirror.

"Damn, Liv." He bites his fist as he looks me over. "You're giving the words "smoke show" a whole new meaning right now."

I blush under his easy praise, wondering if I'll ever get used to the way he sees me.

"It isn't too much?" I ask, turning to inspect the back, uncertainty clear in my voice.

"Were you thinking of wearing less?" The excitement in his expression makes me laugh in spite of my nerves. "Because if you want to take the dress off and stay here, I think it will look just as good on the floor." He waggles his eyebrows. "Maybe even better."

I sigh in mock exasperation at his antics, fighting another smile as I cross the room to the bed so I can sit down to put on my shoes, but he meets me there, kneeling in front of me and kissing each foot before slipping them into the strappy, silver heels himself.

"There." he says softly, looking up at me from the floor with unfiltered adoration. "Now you're absolute perfection."

He stands to help me do the same, and in the high heels, I find myself staring at his bearded chin instead of the usual broad expanse of his chest. His chest that is still exposed by his unbuttoned dress shirt– a deep red, to match my dress. The scent of his skin is intoxicating and without thinking, I lean forward to get closer when the familiar smell has me jerking back again.

"Is that…" I take another whiff, "lavender?" I look at him with my eyebrows drawn before it dawns on me. "Did you use my body wash?"

"I like it when you smell like me." Is his simple, but gruff explanation, and I'm reminded of the very first shower we ever shared together…and then the second.

My cheeks fill with fire.

"Oh," is my amazingly articulate response as we stand staring at each other, remembering things that happened what feels like a lifetime ago.

"Are you ready?" He breaks the spell, and I flick my eyes back up to his.

"Are you?" I counter, gesturing to his still open shirt causing a wolfish grin to spread across his face.

"I can be."

"I don't think so." I respond primly, reaching for the bottom button. His abs twitch beneath my fingertips as I work my way up, but I'll never admit to going slower than necessary just to feel the way his muscles jump under my hands. It's so intimate and erotic, helping each other get dressed like this, and I marvel at how hot putting clothes on someone else can be.

"Are you ready, now?" He breathes the words just inches from my mouth.

"Almost…" I whisper back just before closing the distance.

Jackson

The limo I hired for the evening pulls up to the crumbling curb of the run-down brick building, and the driver gets out to round the vehicle and open the back door. I slide out of the backseat first, holding out a hand for Smokey to follow.

"Where are we?" She asks, concern mingling with curiosity in her tone.

"Welcome to Conjurer's Corner!" I tell her with a flourish of my arm.

She looks around the vacant space, her underwhelmed expression letting me know she's unimpressed, and I have to work to stifle a smile. I did a lot of research before deciding to bring her here, and I know it may not look like much, but she's going to love it.

"Come on, just trust me, Smoke Show." I place my hand on the small of her back guiding her towards the only visible entrance.

The inside is small, and offers even less than the outside, save for two burley, black men sitting in metal folding chairs, playing cards.

"Help you?" The older one says without looking up from his hand. Smokey looks at me expectantly, and it takes all I have to keep from tugging at my shirt collar like a nervous cartoon character.

"Uhh..." I start out, "Bubble, bubble, toil and trouble?" I feel lame saying the password out loud, but the two men smile at each other before scooting their chairs back, and opening what appears to be a hidden door in the concrete floor.

"Go on down," the man who spoke before says, nodding his head towards the stark black opening. Smokey looks at me with questions all over her adorably readable face as I guide her reluctant body forward, but I don't offer any explanations.

"Have fun!" The other guy calls down just before he encloses us in darkness.

"Jackson?" I feel her small hands grip onto me tighter as the door latches above us, sealing us into the stairwell we just entered.

"I'm here, little smoke show."

I take her hand as I tentatively follow the stairs in a downward spiral. Now that my eyes have had a moment to adjust to the darkness, I can pick out dim lights along the ground, showing us where to step.

"Where are we?" Smokey whispers from behind, as if speaking too loudly will shatter the thick silence that surrounds us.

"Almost there," I whisper back just as we come up to another door. This time I knock seven times in a distinctive pattern and the door swings wide to reveal the secret, underground speak-easy I've brought her to.

She gasps audibly as we enter the swanky club, the word *Potions* spelled out in bright edison bulbs above the bar. A woman in silk greets us while another with a voice like velvet croons from the stage that she'll put a spell on us.

As we make our way through the alluring shadows dripping with gold, her head is on a swivel trying to take everything in. The breathless wonder written all over her face is like a drug I will never get enough of.

Once we're seated in a cozy, round booth with a good view of the stage, I encourage her to look over the menu. After smiling over the cleverly named cocktails, she chooses something called, Love Potion Number Nine before getting lost in the surroundings again.

"Do you like it?" I lean in to whisper the question, and my lips brush the shell of her ear.

"Like it?" Her eyes are wide, sparkling with enchanted disbelief. "It's beyond magical. I feel like I fell into some kind of dream!" Then she smiles, and nothing else in the world matters.

Smokey

"Would you like to dance?" Jackson stands and offers me his hand.

"What about our drinks?" I place my palm in his, allowing him to guide me out onto the dance floor.

"They'll be there when we get back." He pulls me close then, twirling me into his embrace with a cocky grin.

When I meet his chest, our bodies press together in a slow, sensual waltz that he leads with practiced skill, making the steps easy to follow. Instead of worrying about where to put my feet, all I can think about is the heat of his body, and the way I can feel his muscles moving and flexing against mine.

Caught up in the music and the way my body comes alive under his hands, I undulate against him, allowing myself to acknowledge how good it feels to be touched by him.

Not just held, but *cradled*. Not just safe, but *seen*. Not just wanted, but *worshipped*.

Jackson makes me feel all of those things at once. He always has.

When the song ends I'm breathless, but it has nothing to do with the dance, and everything to do with the man who leads me back to our private booth where our drinks are indeed waiting.

SMOKE SHOW: A FORBIDDEN AGE GAP ROMANCE

Mine is a dark liquid purple that hombres into a fizzy lavender haze, served in a martini glass with a sugared rim and a maraschino cherry skewer. It looks so whimsical sitting next to his simple crown and coke, but the taste is even better. Like something that should be forbidden; sweet, but with an unexpected edge that lingers on my tongue. It keeps me coming back for more until all of a sudden the glass is empty.

I'm not usually much of a drinker, not fond of the way liquor makes people lose control. I get to see the effects of it all over the city most nights, not just from my past. But when I'm with Jackson, I feel free. Like there's nothing I could do that would push him away. Lord knows I've tried.

Plucking the cherry skewer from the rim, I meet Jackson's gaze as I pull a piece of the alcohol soaked fruit into my mouth. I'm so lost in watching the way his throat works as he swallows, I almost miss the way lust darkens his eyes.

"Would you like another?" He asks, his eyes never leaving my lips as I suck the remaining fruit from the stick. At my nod, Jackson waves two fingers at the waitress, silently signaling for another round.

"How did you find this place?" I ask over the oil lantern flickering between us that causes shadows to dance across the table top the way couples glide across the dance floor.

"I've made a few connections working in the pastry biz these past few months." He shrugs his shoulders then winks at me.

"So what, you delivered cupcakes to the mob and you're like an honorary member now?" I tease and he laughs.

"Something like that."

"Wait, really?" I say, just as the waitress delivers our next round of drinks. As she places them on the table between us, Jackson mimes locking his lips and throwing away the key.

"You're really not going to tell me?"

"If I tell you all of my secrets, then I'd never get to see the way your face lights up like it is right now," he says, and I can feel the blood begin to rush to my face.

"Mmmm," he rumbles, the sound full of unadulterated pleasure, and all the blood that was rushing to my cheeks takes a sudden detour down south as heat floods my core. "I love the way those roses bloom for me, Smokey. Do you think your beautiful bottom would blush as prettily beneath my hands?"

With an audible gulp, I reach for my drink, desperate to douse the fire that's threatening to consume me at the picture he paints with his words. He chuckles at my flustered reaction, the sound slightly sinister as it slides sinfully down my spine, raising goosebumps in its wake.

"Don't worry, Little Smoke Show." He leans in, skating a tantalizing finger down my arm while his whiskey scented breath caresses the side of my face. "I'll wait until you're ready." Then he gently kisses the top of my shoulder before pulling back to continue sipping his drink.

After a few more Love Potions, and several heated glances, all I can think about is how ready I am to strip off this dress and take whatever he can give me.

Jackson

My dick is uncomfortably hard as I carry Smokey back up the stairs to keep her from stumbling. Her shoes dangle from one of my hands as I struggle to open the trap door, but there's no way I'm putting her down.

After she kicked out of her heels at the table, she started on the dress, and I'll be damned if I let her get naked in front of a bunch of strangers. My little Liv is still a light weight, and right now, she is kissing and sucking on my neck while she whispers about how much she misses the way my cock fills her, and I can't seem to get us back to the limo fast enough.

It's dark outside now, but the driver sees us coming and hops out of the driver seat, hastily pulling open the back door. Sliding into the cool leather interior with Smokey on my lap, I nod at the driver signaling for him to close it.

Leaning slightly forward, I reach for the fully stocked mini fridge and pull out a cold bottle of water. Then, sending up a quick prayer for strength, I gently peel Smokey's body from mine. She moans in protest as I make her sit up, already missing the hot, wet suction of her lips against my throat.

"Come on, pretty girl. I know you don't want to, but I need you to sit up and drink some of this for me." Twisting the cap off of the plastic bottle, I hold it to her mouth and help her take a few long pulls of the cool liquid. Some of it dribbles out of the corner of her mouth, and unable to help myself, I lower the bottle so that I can lick the drops away with my tongue.

Her skin is salty and sweet, an intoxicating blend of sugar and sweat. Dragging my tongue down the sensitive column of her throat, she shifts in my lap, straddling me, and grasps my head in her hands, holding me to her as she plunges her fingers into my hair.

"More." She gasps out. "I need more." Pulling my mouth from her overheated flesh, her lips find mine in a ravenous kiss that has her sucking on my tongue and nipping at my bottom lip like she can't get enough. Then she begins to rock on top of me, unconsciously grinding her hot little pussy against my erection in a mindless search for release. I can feel her arousal soaking through my slacks, and I know my resolve isn't going to last much longer.

"Smokey, baby..." I mumble against her lips, trying to gently shift her off of me, just a little. "We can't do this here. Not like this." I finally have her attention, as she leans back to pout at me.

"Why not?"

"Because you're drunk, Little Smoke Show." I brush a few curls back from her face to soften the sting of the rejection I'm sure she's feeling. "And I don't want to take advantage of the situation."

"But...what if I want you to?"

"Smokey, I..." I flounder, my voice pained. "I can't risk messing this up again."

"Then don't." She whispers it against my lips just before kissing me as if she can drink me in. When she finally pulls away to catch her breath, I rest my forehead against hers.

"I don't want you to hate me." I whisper, fear dripping off the same words we said to each other two and a half years ago.

Framing my face in her hands, Smokey looks into my eyes, allowing me to see how clear hers are, despite the alcohol warming her blood.

"Jackson I..." she falters for a moment before I see determination flash in her eyes. "I could never hate you. Because I'm in love with you."

I stop breathing and she goes on.

"I tried convincing myself it was wrong, but the only thing that makes sense to me is you. I'm more myself when you're around than when you're not. You make me feel all sorts of things I've never felt before but most of all...most of all, you make me feel free. So please," she looks at me with hope in her eyes, "don't hold back on me now. Not anymore. I want it all, everything you promised me...Okay? Jackson?" She prompts, uncertainty creeping into her voice when I still haven't said anything.

Then, without warning, I pull her forward, crushing her into me.

"I love you too." I murmur against her skin, trailing kisses anywhere they can reach as she squeals with surprised laughter.

"Prove it." The little vixen whispers devilishly into my ear as she reaches between us and begins unfastening my belt.

When she has my pants unbuttoned and my dick springs free, I stroke it a few times while she watches, her dilated eyes tracking every inch my hand travels. When a bead of pre-cum forms at the tip, she licks her lips hungrily, as if she can't wait to taste it.

"You want this dick, Little Smoke Show?" I grunt as I pleasure myself in front of her. She nods eagerly, never lifting her eyes from my shaft. "You want it to stretch out your tight little cunt while you writhe and beg me to fuck you?" My voice gets deeper as I pump my fist up and down.

"Yes, please, Jackson. I need it." She whimpers, wiggling around on my lap, searching for the right kind of friction to make herself feel good.

"Come and show me who it belongs to, then." I challenge her, and with one last stroke, she's bunching her dress up around her waist as she lifts up onto her knees and lines her dripping pussy up with my aching cock. With a loud, drawn out moan, she sits on my dick, filling herself with the appendage in one smooth motion.

"Fuck!" The expletive bursts from me as her pussy flutters around my cock, adjusting to the sudden intrusion. "You're so tight, Smokey, I can feel your heartbeat." She moans again, her inner walls spasming at my words, choking my dick even more.

"It only beats for youuuu..." She drags the last word out in ecstasy as she lifts herself up and then sinks back down again, riding me in a slow, steady rhythm that has us both seeing stars. Or maybe that's just the blur of streetlights passing us by, who knows. All I care about is the way her pussy grips me, and the way she begs me for each thrust.

I can't tell if the way she pants my name is a request or a demand, but either way I know I'll give her whatever she's asking for. Gripping her hips, I slide down in the seat a little, giving myself more leverage and depth, causing her to cry out when I thrust in again. It's deeper, thanks to the new angle, and I can feel the way my cock kisses her cervix as I bottom out inside her. Her pussy clamps around me, even while she complains that it's too much.

"But you can take it anyway, can't you Little Smoke Show?" I taunt her as I fuck her, "Take it all, and ask for more?"

"Yes, Jackson, yes! Give me more!" She moans as she bounces on my cock now, chasing after her release in earnest.

"That's right, baby. Take what you need from me." I tell her, and as if on command, she comes all around me, milking me dry in the process.

It feels like we've transcended time, but as the waves of pleasure recede and we catch our breath, we both become very aware that the vehicle is no longer moving.

"How long have we..." She trails off without finishing the question.

"I don't know, and I don't care." I tell her truthfully. "I'll pay to have the limo detailed if I have to." She smiles and I can only imagine how red her cheeks are right now.

"Still," she says, "maybe we should apologize or something."

"Absolutely not." I tell her as I rebutton my pants and rescue my belt from the floor. "I'll never apologize for giving you exactly what you want." I say as I open the door and step out to find the driver already standing there, leaning against the long black car.

When he sees me, he straightens, offering a bland, professional expression as if he didn't just hear me and my girl come undone in the backseat.

"Will there be anything else, sir?" He asks as I hold a hand out for Smokey to make her exit.

"Nope." I tell him, slapping a hundred dollar bill into his palm with a large, shit-eating grin.

Smokey

"Come on, it was fun! Admit it."

"She said all my hair is going to fall out! How does that sound like fun to you?"

I laugh at Jackson as we leave the little fortune-teller's shop where Madame Simone had some very interesting predictions today, to say the least.

"Think of all the money you're going to save on shampoo, though!" I cackle. "Every reading has a silver lining, you know."

"Oh yeah? Maybe she meant that all my facial hair would fall out. See how you like that silver lining." I gasp in immediate horror at his words.

"You bite your tongue!"

We laugh together as we stroll down the sidewalk hand in hand, until he tugs me to a stop in front of a window that says *NOLA Tattoo*.

"You wanna?" He tilts his head towards the building.

"Get a tattoo?" I can't hide the surprise in my voice. "Are you serious?" Nervous excitement bubbles up inside me at the idea. I've always kind of wanted a tattoo. Especially after spending so much time admiring all of Jackson's.

"Yeah, why not? Unless, ya know, you're too scared or whatever." He shrugs nonchalantly like it's no big deal.

"Jackson Henry Holloway, I *know* you did not just insinuate that I am afraid of a little needle."

"Of course not, Little Smoke Show. I'm not insinuating anything." He says the words, but the smirk on his face and the glimmer in his eyes are definitely calling me chicken.

"If you can do it, I can do it." I raise my chin with pride, even while my stomach fills with nerves. What if it really hurts and I act like a baby in front of my boyfriend?

"Oh yeah?" He quirks an eyebrow. "How about we make things a little more interesting, then?" My anxious stomach drops, but I can't deny my rising excitement and interest. I've always wanted to get a tattoo, and I know Jackson would never make a suggestion like this if he didn't think I could handle it.

"What do you have in mind?" I ask cautiously.

"You let me pick out your first tattoo." Ughh, the audacity of this man, I swear.

"What? That's crazy! I should get to pick my first one."

"Do you trust me, Little Smoke Show?" It's a simple question, but a loaded one.

"Always." I respond immediately, and he smiles like he just won something.

"Prove it." He smugly says the words I said to him in the back of a limo two days ago, and I narrow my eyes at him.

"That's dirty."

"Maybe." He shrugs. "But I bet it worked, didn't it?" I roll my eyes at him before grabbing his hand.

"Let's just get this over with."

"That's my girl." He praises just before kissing the top of my head and following me inside.

The interior is dimly lit, and the loud, electronic buzzing of a tattoo gun drowns out the sound of classic rock playing softly through hidden speakers.

"Welcome to *NOLA Tattoo*, be right with you!" a disembodied voice shouts from behind a black curtain. Neither one of us bothers to offer a response, as we observe the samples of artwork on display all over the establishment. As I look at all the complex and colorful designs, I can't help but wonder what Jackson has in store for me.

"What can I do for you folks?" A guy who looks like the off-brand version of Willie Nelson emerges from behind a black curtain to greet us.

"Yes, sir, we'd both like tattoos, but I've got to warn you, we're going to be a little unconventional about it." Jackson speaks up, so I don't have to. Talking to new people, especially men, can be difficult for me.

"Is that right?" The man asks, wiping his hands on a stained rag. His slight lisp and missing front teeth remind me of Lenny, and Jackson's voice fades out while he explains our arrangement to the man.

An odd pang of grief ripples through me as I recall the way the old cashier was kind to me when no one else was, and I send up a quick prayer that he's doing okay.

"Who's goin' first?"

The Willie Nelson look-a-like asks, his eyes bouncing back and forth between us.

"She is–"

"He is–"

We answer in unison, and the artist stares at us lamely, silently telling us to get our shit together. Jackson turns to me.

"It's gotta be you, Smoke Show."

"Why? Watching you go first could be really comforting, though. Show me that it's not that bad." I try to rationalize with him.

"Because I have a plan." He tells me, stroking the hair back from my face. "And you said you trust me."

I bite my lip as I consider the situation. I know if I change my mind, Jackson won't hold it against me. He'll just wait patiently until I'm ready. Knowing that makes it easy to give him what he wants.

"Okay." I nod, and he kisses the top of my head again.

"You're so brave, Smokey. I'm so proud of you."

The tension I've been carrying since we walked in evaporates under the warm fuzzies his words evoke, and I know I made the right call. "Let me just talk to him about what I'm thinking so he can get it drawn up for you." At my dubious expression he cups my face in his hands. "I promise, it won't take long, and you won't regret it." Then he plants a quick, but possessive kiss on my lips before disappearing with Willie-Lite.

It's barely been ten minutes when Jackson reappears to tell me that they're ready for me. He guides me behind the counter, through the curtain, and into a small cubicle across from another where a woman with a face full of piercings is inking a fierce blue panther with yellow eyes onto someone's back. Lost in the artwork, I don't notice the blindfold until it's too late.

"Wait, what the hell? Jackson?" My hands fly up to the bandana covering my eyes just as it's cinched tight behind my head.

"It's alright, Smokey, it's just to keep you from seeing the design when he lays the template on your skin. You can't see it until it's finished."

"I didn't agree to that!"

"I told you I have a plan. Plus, I'll be here the whole time."

"You promise?" My voice trembles slightly, displaying how vulnerable the loss of one of my senses makes me. I feel Jackson's big, warm hands envelope mine just before his lips place gentle kisses to the backs of each one.

"I'm not going anywhere. I promise."

"Are you ready?" The unfamiliar voice of the artist cuts in, and I nod my head, unable to speak around the lump forming in my throat.

To my surprise, the design is much smaller than I anticipated, and barely takes any time at all. It's in an odd place as well. Certainly not the spot I would have chosen for my first tattoo, which only peaks my curiosity even more. It barely even hurt, and I feel kind of silly now for being so scared before. I've definitely been through worse.

"Can I see it yet?" I ask, practically bouncing in the seat with excitement.

"In just a second, be still." Jackson admonishes me with a squeeze of his hand.

"Alright, that'll do her." Roger, the tattoo artist says just as something passes over the sensitive skin of my ring finger, causing it to sting uncomfortably for a moment.

"*Now* can I see?" I ask impatiently, eager to pull the blindfold off.

"Yeah, Smoke Show. Now you can look."

Without hesitation, I push the blindfold up until it falls off my head completely and stare down at the loopy symbol that now lives permanently on my left hand. Even though I recognize it, confusion is plain on my face when I look at Jackson and find him kneeling before me.

"Smokey...I love you. And there isn't any amount of time or distance that can change that. Lord knows we tried." He smiles a little, but it doesn't reach his eyes as he gulps, and for the first time, I notice how unsure of himself he seems.

"Jackson–" I start to comfort him when he blurts out, "Will you marry me?"

Stunned silence fills the space between us.

"What did you just say?" I ask dumbly.

"Uhmm..." He shifts at my feet. "I said I love you, and I want to spend the rest of my life with you. What do you say?"

Jackson

"**H**old on, let me get this straight." She stares down at the swirling infinity symbol I had drawn up just for her. "You let me agree to this *before* you popped the question?" She glares at me, her tone accusatory.

Shit, this wasn't how it was supposed to go.

"Well, I..." I flounder for an explanation, as panic seizes my lungs.

Then she smiles, a mischievous gleam in her eyes as she slides out of the chair and saunters towards me.

"I swear, Jackson, those impulses of yours are going to get you into some real trouble, one day." She stops in front of me. "But not today." Then her lips are on mine, kissing me with an urgency I easily match.

"So, that's a *yes*?" I ask against her lips, needing the clarification after the stunt she just pulled.

"Only if you get one, too." She holds up her left hand to indicate the new tattoo at the base of her ring finger.

"Deal."

THE BURN OF THE NEEDLE moving in and out of my flesh is therapeutic, and I find myself being lulled almost to sleep by the soothing vibration. Time flies as he grinds the metal tip into my skin, and all too soon, Roger is finished. The cloth is rough against my newly sensitive skin as he wipes up the remaining ink and blood that oozes from the fresh artwork.

"What do you think?" he asks before I hear Smokey shuffle closer for a better look. The symbols are mirror images of each other, with Smokey's being slightly more delicate to fit her smaller finger.

"It's fucking perfect," I growl possessively as I grab the woman who inspired the creation. "Do you know that?" I ask right before I kiss her senseless. "*You* are fucking perfect. And now you're mine forever. There's nowhere you could ever go that I wouldn't follow or find you."

"Is that a threat?" She asks, and I squeeze her tight, burying my face in her curls as she laughs, and for the first time in my life, I feel like my past isn't hanging over me, taunting me with a future I'll never have.

Everything I need is already right here in my arms.

"Absolutely."

The End

Epilogue

Jackson

"**J**ackson, get out! It's bad luck to see the cake before the wedding!" My fiancée shrieks at me as I saunter into the bakery kitchen.

"Actually, it's the dress you're thinking of, Smoke Show." I wink at her, which causes her to flush the way I love before she rolls those big, blue orbs in her head at me.

"Not for *our* wedding!" she says back with exasperation. "Annette is actually trusting me to make the cake on my own, and I have a vision. It's important to me."

"That's exactly why I'm here." I dip my finger into a large, silver mixing bowl left discarded on the counter. "If it's important to you, then it's important to me." I suck the cake batter off of my finger, punctuating my last statement with a pop as I pull it from my lips. She pretends to glare at me for a moment before deflating.

"It's important to me to do it on my own." She huffs out a breath as she turns to face me fully. She looks adorable with a smudge of flour on her nose, or it could be powdered sugar. The way she eats beignets, you'd never know. "I love that you want to be a part of this with me, but this is what I've been working towards."

"I know, love." I pull her into a hug so that I have an excuse to touch her. Burying my nose in her hair, I inhale the scent of her sweat mixed with lavender and a hint of cocoa.

"I want to surprise *you* more than anyone else." She mumbles self-consciously against my chest.

"Smokey..." I tip her chin up so that she has no choice but to look me in the eyes. "I'm surprised by you every day." I caress the side of her face with reverence, tracing my thumb along her plump lower lip. "Don't you know that?" The lip in question begins to tremble slightly. "Every morning I wake up, and see you sleeping next to me, I'm surprised. The way you sing in the shower when you think no one else is home. The way you can drink a gallon of hot bean water a day, and still fall asleep at night. That's all surprising." She laughs despite the tears glistening in her eyes. "Every time you laugh," I smile at her in wonder. "That surprises the hell out of me." I see the question forming in her eyes. "The world has given you so many reasons not to laugh...so every time you do...it's like fucking magic. It heals parts of me I didn't even know were broken. And *that's* surprising. You are the most wonderful surprise of my life every single day simply because you exist." True to the word, she launches herself at me, climbing me like a vine before sealing her decadent mouth to mine in a sudden, scorching kiss.

The way her tongue moves against mine has me thinking of ways to get her naked and covered in chocolate, but as if she can read my thoughts, she pulls away, releasing me and melting my fantasies like the sweet candy I want her coated in.

"I love you. So much." I take great pleasure in her disheveled appearance and breathless declaration. "But you definitely have to go, or else I won't get any work done." She attempts to turn me in the direction of the exit so she can shoo me out of the kitchen, but her petite form is no match for my much larger frame. I might as well be a mountain as far as she's concerned.

"I don't know, Smoke Show. You just made a very convincing argument for me to stay." I cross my arms smugly over my chest.

"Jackson, *please*," she begs, changing tactics. "I'll make you breakfast in bed tomorrow, but you have to go *now*." She tugs on one of my arms, attempting to drag me the way she wants me to go.

"Hmm..." I stroke my chin, pretending to consider her offer, barely having to work to resist her efforts. "Will you serve me my breakfast wearing only your apron?" I smile salaciously at her and she stops, blinking at me as her cheeks turn rosy, stunned by the proposition. I love doing that to her.

"Fine. However you want it, just please get out of here, so I can focus and get back to work."

"You got yourself a deal, Liv." I feel my smile turn feral at her words as I finally allow her to push me from the room.

Smokey

IT'S BEEN HECTIC LATELY, prepping and baking for the wedding, but I still managed to pull myself from Jackson's cozy embrace before the ass crack of dawn in order to keep my side of the bargain we struck yesterday. He didn't want to let me go at first, but when I reminded him of why, all I got was a deep, gravelly chuckle followed by a self-satisfied, "Bring me my breakfast, wench!" before he released me with a slap on the ass. I may have huffed with the pretense of annoyance as I threw on my robe, but truthfully, I'm delighted. I've never had a better reason to wake up early in all my life.

Rather than banging around in our tiny kitchen upstairs, I head down into *La Petite* to first check on my cake frosting before taking advantage of the space and state-of-the-art appliances. Jackson will try every frilly, fancy pastry I ask him to, but when it comes to his own tastes, he's a simple, meat-and-potatoes kind of guy. It was with that thought in mind that I remembered to grab a steak out of the freezer before going to bed last night, so that it could thaw out while I slept.

I find real joy in cooking, in the creation of something beautiful that I can tell tastes good by the reactions that play out over someone's face. It's like I'm creating living art; not out of the food, though the presentation can definitely feel that way. I mean out of the people, and the way they respond to my food. Their reactions—*That's* the real artistry. Only once I've made myself a strong cup of the Lord's elixir will I begin with the food prep, though.

Even though I know he'd prefer a ribeye, I set the dregs of my unfinished coffee to the side to unwrap the New York strip from its white butcher paper, seasoning it with salt and pepper before setting it aside to prep the potatoes. Once those are washed, cubed, and chilling in an ice bath, I fry up about a pound of bacon. After I have each strip crisped to perfection and drip-draining on a rack, I retrieve the potatoes, draining and drying them as best I can before adding them to the still hot bacon grease, doing my best not to splash myself with the hot, bubbling oil.

While they fry, I return my attention to the steak, searing both sides of it in a cast iron skillet before finishing it off with a pat of seasoned butter and placing the whole thing into the oven. As the meat finishes, I strain the fried potatoes from the sizzling bacon grease and set them on a platter to cool alongside the bacon. All that's left is retrieving the steak from the oven so it can rest while I grab a couple of croissants and allow a generous amount of honey butter to melt over them, creating a sweet and sticky glaze. Once I've assembled the large spread onto a wooden serving tray, I grab a roll of silverware and swipe a Red Bull from the box in the fridge that I keep on hand just for him because he hates coffee, yet has a caffeine addiction that rivals mine.

That's not something I knew about him before. I smile a little to myself at all the little ways we've grown together these last few months. At all the ways we've only grown closer, and more sure of each other, despite the many obstacles we face due to prejudices about our age difference and the way we met. Not to mention the way society generally treats ex-cons.

But I don't care about any of it—what anyone thinks or says. I've been to Hell and back already, and there isn't anyone or anything on this plane of existence that can separate me from the truth I know in my heart: Jackson and I were meant for each other, and I love him with an intensity that words fall short of expressing. The best part is, I know he loves and accepts me the same way, too. I know it with a surety that I think only comes from finding one's soulmate.

Stopping just outside my bedroom door, I set the tray down as quietly as possible to disrobe. Leaving the velvety satin fabric in a pale blue puddle on the floor, I pick the tray back up and quietly re-enter the bedroom wearing nothing but a short, black apron tied around my waist.

Bonus Content

Craving more heat?

Visit adrylandwritesromance.com for exclusive access to an extended epilogue that includes more spice from Jackson's POV.

What's Next?

While Smoke Show was contemporary, A. D. Ryland is still developing as an author, and is excited to dive into her plans for a dystopian fantasy world, complete with a cursed FMC, and the entity that can hear her thoughts and taste her feelings.

If you like: fated mates, discovering your true nature, and getting sweet revenge, you won't want to miss it.

Queen of The Hollow coming fall of 2026.

Acknowledgements

First and foremost, I want to thank my husband. Not just for the amazing cover art (if you didn't already know, Mr. Ryland drew that by hand), but also for his continuous, unending support of my dream. This book and these characters (specifically Jackson) would not exist without you, my love.

I also want to give a shout out to my kids who have absolutely no business reading this book. If you did, I don't want to hear it. You were warned.

I'm sorry for the moments it felt like you had to go without while I chased my happiness. I hope, in the process, you learned to trust in yourself and the things that set your soul on fire. Most of the time, the only thing standing in your way is Y.O.U.

To the friends that acted as sounding boards and critique partners, I don't think there is a word strong enough to describe what you mean to me. Mia, Kat, and Lacey, you all kept me focused and helped me see the forest whenever I was lost in the trees. Toby, Parrish, Cam, and Alice, your unwavering faith in me was fuel when I wanted to give up and let the imposter syndrome win.

To my alphas and my betas, though there weren't many of you, the feedback each of you gave helped guide Smoke Show to what it is now, and I'm so so grateful for all of you.

As for my family, I want to thank my older sister for reading one of my short stories when we were young, and telling me that if it had more dialogue it would actually be pretty good. I didn't know what the word meant at the time, and to be honest, I still don't know if I'm any good at writing it. You'll have to let me know.

Lastly, I want to thank my dad. When I was growing up, sure I wanted to be a singer, or a doctor, or maybe a journalist, he looked at me and said, "I think you'll be a writer." Smut probably isn't what you had in mind, but your words still held power that day.

I hope I make you proud.

About The Author

Though her heart belongs to the magical, moss-draped swamps of Louisiana, author **A.D. Ryland** currently resides in Oklahoma, where she lives with her husband, youngest son, and an unruly pack of four-legged fur babies, including two spoiled Great Danes and a golden Lab/Pit mix.

As a wife, mother, and creator, Ryland knows everything is a balancing act. She divides her time between writing steamy romance, editing her own chaos, marketing her books, and figuring out what the hell to make for dinner...every single night...forever.

When she's not putting her characters through emotional trauma (or herself through a Chloe Ting workout), you can find her sipping matcha, daydreaming about writing enough smut to fund a sustainable, off-grid life in a custom-built hobbit house—complete with chickens, bees, a greenhouse, and a revolving door of rescued dogs.